the
impossible
dinosaur

The Impossible Dinosaur
has been specially
commissioned for Tesco

Cover Illustration Andy Parker

Published by
Tesco Stores Limited
Created by Brilliant Books Ltd
84-86 Regent Street
London WIB 5RR

First Published 2001

Printed by Lego Print S.P.A
Reproduction by Colourpath, England

1 3 5 7 9 10 8 6 4 2

the impossible dinosaur

Glenn Dakin

CHAPTER ONE

Sharing a home with fourteen thousand dinosaur bones can be quite tricky. It can certainly be annoying trying to find space for all of them. Rose Morrow was finding that moving house with a whole private prehistoric museum was almost impossible. Especially when you felt miserable and had never wanted to move in the first place.

Rose was shattered. The long carriage ride from their old home in Lyme Regis had left her shaken, and now she was faced with chaos in their new home. Delivery men were carting boxes back and forth, while Agatha, the housemaid, ran to and from the waterpump in the street so that she could heat water over the kitchen fire and start scrubbing the filthy floors. The gaslamp in the dark hallway would not work, so Rose walked through into the conservatory to study her father's complicated drawing of where everything should go.

"Ahem. Pardon me, miss," coughed one of the delivery men politely. "Where would you be wantin' this Per-

Terry-Dacker-Tile?"

"That's pterodactyl," corrected Rose patiently. "And could you bring it through here to me? The instructions are very clear. Large Flying Lizards in the conservatory, Marine Reptiles in the study, and Ammonites and other Prehistoric Shellfish in the drawing room."

"Sorry, ma'am, 'ow silly of me," the old removal man smiled to himself, before turning and bellowing to his three assistants. "Per-Terry-Dacker-Tile, five large crates of, through 'ere, right now!"

Rose sat on a pile of boxes and looked at the official delivery list the man had left for Papa to sign. At the top it said, 'October 12th 1891'. She fixed the date in her mind. Today, her happy world back in Lyme Regis had been left behind for ever. Now they would begin their new life in the great city of London. How it scared her.

She looked at herself in an ornate mirror that was lying at a lop-sided angle against the wall. Her long dark plaits framed her sad face and made her look paler than ever. Where was Papa when she needed him? Her father, Stanley Morrow, was a respected scientist and collector, an expert on fossils. Yet whenever there was any real organising to be done he seemed to disappear. Her mother had been the great one for getting things done, Rose sighed. But she never let herself think about Mama.

"The professor says it's some sort of monstrosity with

wings," yelled a young delivery lad who had tracked her father down studying plant specimens in the front garden – away from all the hullaballoo of moving. "'E didn't know where it went, though!"

"Then bring it through 'ere," shouted back the old man. "Flying Lizards is for the conservatory, madam says. Any problem with that?"

"All right, all right," grumbled, the young lad. "Except that there ain't no such thing as a Flying Lizard."

Rose laughed despite herself. The discovery of the great and ancient family of dinosaurs was still so new that hardly any people – well, ordinary people – knew any-thing about them. It always seemed incredible to Rose how little interest most people took in nature.

She wandered out into the dreary little garden, and peered up at the house. It was tall, dark and frightening against the grey autumn sky. She shivered. There was that touch of yellow in the misty air that she had noticed when they reached the edge of London. That scared her, too. She had heard all kinds of stories about the thick London fogs that made you ill. She tried not to breathe in, then scowled.

"I can't spend the rest of my life not breathing!" she said to herself, angrily. "Oh, I just know I'm going to feel wretched here!"

If only Papa's job hadn't brought him to this cold, grey

city. Why did London have to become the Fossil Capital of the World? It was already the capital of everything else. It wasn't fair. It wasn't as if any of the fossils were ever found in London. Most of them were found in Lyme Regis! But grown-ups always had to get everything upside down.

She went back into the house and heard her father fussing in the hallway. "Well, this is extraordinary!" he declared. "Quite, quite impossible!" Rose's father never really got angry – in fact, he was rather a timid man. For him to be speaking like this meant he must be very upset.

"Don't worry, sir," said one of the removal lads. "It'll turn up! These things always 'appens with removals. We've lost thousands of things…"

"Ahem!" interrupted the old boss. "What my young assistant means, Professor Morrow, is that we've never lost anything. But to the inexpert eye, things look lost… until they is found!" he remarked brightly.

Rose poked her head round the hall door. "What is it, Papa? Are you all right?"

"It's only my most precious chest of all!" he whispered to her. "The one I told you about… my Greatest Discovery!"

"You mean the Unknown Fossil?" she replied quietly. "The one even *you* couldn't identify?"

"Yes!" hissed Stanley, glancing over his shoulder

nervously to make sure the removal men weren't listening. "That set of bones is unlike anything ever seen before by science! It will become the most famous mystery of the age!"

"But, I thought I saw it arrive, Papa, on the second cart…"

Suddenly the old boss burst through the door, waving a sheet at them. "'Ere we go, guv'nor! 'Ere's the matter, all in writin'. Morrow Household, Job 3, Cart 4B, Load 2. Perticklers: Cargo called 'Skeleton X', a collection of Dino-Saurus Fossils, packed in thirteen numbered chests." He led them into the front garden, where a great stack of boxes was ready to be taken indoors.

"That's just it!" Professor Morrow blurted out in a high-pitched squeak. "I've counted over and over again, and there are only twelve chests! The final chest… the most important one, is missing!"

A silence fell on the scene. The removal man took off his glasses and rubbed his eyes slowly.

"Missin'? That's not a word we like to hear in the Removal Trade – a business that is quite as ancient and respectable an enterprise as the Dino-Saurus Business." He tapped his inventory sheet and strode off. "I'll check with the office!"

Rose's father suddenly seemed very tired. He sank into

an old leather armchair that had also been left in the front garden.

"The thirteenth chest! We must find it!" he whispered.

Just then, one of the younger workmen wandered by.

"Thirteen chests you say," the lad remarked. "It's unlucky ain't it? Twelve chests is all right... but some people don't like shifting an unlucky number. Someone probably took that thirteenth chest off the cart... deliberate!"

Unlucky – Rose felt unlucky all right. That evening her new bedroom was icy cold and she could see her breath in front of her face. Agatha would be heating up a bag of oats in the oven for Rose to put into her bed to warm it up.

In her nightgown she peered out of the window down into the street. The lamplighter had been by, and the gaslamps made the fog look even yellower than before. It must be incredibly cold, Rose thought, because there was a man in the street below so bundled up in cloaks and scarves that not an inch of his face could be seen. He seemed to be studying their house. He was probably just curious about the new arrivals.

Rose couldn't sleep very well in her unfamiliar bed. She got up hours later and went to look out of the window again. She was amazed to see the man was still there. Hidden by the curtains, she gazed in wonder at the motionless man. Had he really been staring at their house all that time? Rose felt uneasy.

"How could any human being stand completely still for so long in such freezing weather?" she wondered to herself. She shivered and dived back under her covers.

CHAPTER TWO

"Well if you didn't do it, Rosemary, who did?" Rose's father asked, peering through his half-moon glasses at her.

They were both in the study looking at a scene of upheaval. Last night, Professor Morrow had made an effort to put the room in some kind of order. Now they were met with a curious topsy-turvy scene. Piles of boxes had been knocked over, jars and cases had tumbled down on all sides, and rolled-up charts were scattered across the floor.

"Thieves!" Rose cried out.

"There are no signs of any forced entry, and absolutely nothing has been taken," her father said, baffled.

"But look, Papa! All the special chests – they've been moved!"

It was true. On closer inspection, it seemed that someone had been pulling and pushing the twelve chests that contained Skeleton X. It was the attempts to wrestle these heavy boxes out of various corners that had led to everything else being knocked aside.

"They've all been dragged towards each other!" Rose said, puzzled. "Look – someone has started to pull them together!"

She was hurt that her father could possibly think she might be behind such odd behaviour. "If nobody broke in, then perhaps the house is haunted!" she blurted out.

"Well, my dear," said her father. "I can see that my many years of teaching you to seek sensible scientific explanations have been completely wasted."

Rose was upset. "But Papa, if I study the fossils I always put everything back carefully – you know I do! I would never create a mess like this!"

"Yes, yes," he replied, in a kinder tone, but his face showed a weary strain. "It is just possible, you know, that since your poor mother died you have become so taken over by all this…" he gestured around the room, "by my work, my fossils, my dinosaurs… that you may have come down here in your sleep, and got up to who knows what, quite unaware of what you were doing!"

"But Papa!" protested Rose indignantly. " I wouldn't even have the strength to move those cases!"

"You do hear funny tales about sleepwalkers…" he began. Then he shook his head. "No, now I am being ridiculous. What a worry this all is!"

Just then Agatha bustled in and handed a card to

Professor Morrow.

"Gentleman caller!" she said, with a special emphasis on the 'gentleman' as if the arrival really was rather impressive.

Stanley went to the door and was astonished to find none other than Sir Gordon Bowler, Head of the Natural History Museum, waiting there. He was a handsome man with a trim black moustache, in a smart grey frock coat and immaculate white gloves. He was very young to be the head of a museum, Rose thought, keeping her place in the shadows, far behind her father. Behind Sir Gordon, the four horses that drove his carriage tossed their heads haughtily, as if wondering whether this neighbourhood was quite good enough for them.

"Good day to you, Professor Morrow, or may I call you Stanley? I just thought I'd drop by and see if you had settled nicely into your new nest!" Professor Morrow was flabbergasted at the honour of a visit from such a great personage, and could hardly utter a reply.

"I'm so looking forward to your lecture! What is its title, now? A most interesting one – 'The Impossible Dinosaur'! Very exciting it all sounds. I take it that all your specimens have arrived safely? No bones broken, I hope?" he chuckled softly.

Stanley finally found his voice.

"Well, Sir... I am sorry to say that one of my boxes –

14

one of the most important ones – has disappeared! It's all most worrying," he confessed nervously. "I was just thinking of writing you a note to suggest I postpone my lecture until a later date."

Sir Gordon fell silent. Stanley's words seemed to have upset him. "Well!" he exclaimed, tapping his walking stick against his boot irritably. "Well, this *is* disappointing!"

"I'm sure we'll find it soon!" Professor Morrow said.

"This does cause problems..." Sir Gordon murmured to himself, as if lost in thought. Suddenly he snapped out of it, and pointed at Professor Morrow with the tip of his expensive cane.

"Our invitation for you to join our Natural History Society was made largely because of your promise to show us a truly unique dinosaur. Now, as soon as you arrive in London, you claim that part of your discovery has vanished into thin air!"

Professor Morrow was lost for words. Sir Gordon carried on, seeming really very put out.

"Now listen, Professor Morrow! Many tricksters have invented tall stories in an attempt to join our society before now, you know. I hope you won't turn out to be one of them!" he sniffed, and was off. It was an awful moment, and as his horses drew away, their whinnying sounded like mocking laughter in Rose's ears.

Rose's father shrank back indoors, suddenly looking

old and worried. Agatha brought him a cup of lemon tea, which he sipped, shaking, slumped in his favourite chair.

"It's disaster upon disaster!" he wailed. "If that thirteenth chest doesn't turn up soon, I shall be ruined! Why haven't we heard from those delivery men?"

Professor Morrow had hoped that his lecture would be the start of a brilliant career in the great city. The interest from the famous museum had been one of the things that had encouraged him to move to London. Now his confidence had collapsed like a house of cards.

The dreary day passed slowly. Her father had not found a school for Rose yet, so she was teaching herself from a great pile of books about fossils. Instead of finding this arrangement boring, Rose thought it was ideal. She loved learning, and would rather teach herself about her beloved dinosaurs than learn mathematics and grammar at school. Alone, she lost herself in a gigantic volume about the Silurian Epoch. While her mind recorded the bare facts, her imagination roamed off into the incredible world of the past. Soon she began to feel happier.

She decided that even in this miserable city there must be some wildlife for her to study. The London gloom had hardly given them any light all day, and now, as she looked out into the garden in the late afternoon, it felt almost like night. Rose peered around, but try as she might she could find no sign of life in her new garden. Not a crow nor a stray cat could be seen. From time to time she would put down her book and look out again, but not a single sparrow hopped into view. In the end she gave up reading altogether and simply stared out of the window. Time ticked by, but absolutely no living thing would come anywhere near to their house. It was most peculiar.

Then she saw him again. Advancing up the road in the murky twilight was the man she had seen last night. He walked slowly, almost creeping at a snail's pace. She raced downstairs.

"It's him! He's back!" Rose cried. Her father gave her a puzzled look, and told her to calm down. Rose gulped.

"Papa, last night I saw a funny man, in a sort of disguise, staring at our house for ages! Well, now he's back! Papa, you must call the police. I can't bear to think of him standing there outside all night again!"

"Yes, yes, I did actually notice him myself yesterday," Professor Morrow said. "I suppose he could have been a sort of 'look-out man', or whatever such criminals call themselves. Well, it might be nothing, but perhaps I will bring him to the attention of the authorities. I'll get my cloak and go out the back way. Now, now, Rose, leave grown-up matters to me, and don't run about the house shrieking!"

He set off without delay and Rose returned, slightly miffed, to her room. Wrapped in a blanket and wearing her gloves, she picked up her fossil book and, under the gaslamp, turned to a new page. It was strange, she thought, finding it hard to concentrate. Bringing the police in should make her feel safer. Yet somehow it just made her feel as if they really were in some kind of danger.

CHAPTER THREE

"Rose!"

This time Stanley Morrow was not accusing his daughter of anything. He simply wanted her to share an extraordinary sight with him. He had opened up his study door the next morning to behold something incredible.

The twelve chests – so carefully tidied away the previous day – had been dragged from their places again. They were all gathered together in the centre of the room, some standing on their sides, some leaning against each other, like a miniature Stonehenge.

But strangest of all, was... what had happened to the bones. They were everywhere, on top of the cases, poking out from under lids, or lying on the floor. Some had been fitted together. Part of a gruesome skull had been assembled on top of a case, and a great dark hollow eye stared back at the astonished Morrows.

Rose gasped as she looked down at her feet and saw

fragments of a terrible dark claw, put together jigsaw-fashion at her feet. It seemed to be pointing menacingly towards her.

Professor Morrow was distraught.

"My fossils! My precious bones!" he wailed. He began to fuss around, putting everything back where it belonged. Even after they had checked the room thoroughly, they were faced with the same mystery as before. Again there was no sign of entry, and again nothing had been stolen. Professor Morrow was exasperated. He flew about the room, tidying and snapping at Agatha, who was trying to help.

"It's some sort of extraordinary prank – it must be!" he muttered. "I don't know why I called on the police last night, I really don't!" he said to himself. "They were supposed to watch the house! What good did it do?"

Rose knew when to make herself scarce. She went out into the garden, to hide until the house calmed down again. She stood in the chilly air, once again disappointed by the complete absence of wildlife all around her. Agatha had optimistically started a birdtable, and some crumbs had been put out, but there were no cheerful feathered visitors.

"Is there really no nature in London, or is it just our house?" she asked herself. Then she heard someone bouncing a ball against the wall next door. Suddenly it struck her how nice it would be to make a friend.

"Hello!" she called out to whoever it was on the other side. "I can hear you playing – but I can't see you!" The ball stopped bouncing. There was a long silence. Rose tried again. "Hello there? Who are you? I… I just wanted to say hello, because I haven't got any friends here, you see."

There was another pause. Then a girl's voice said, "No friends at all?"

"None," began Rose. "You see we've just –"

"Then you must be positively frightful!" exclaimed the voice, and ran away. Rose felt dejected. Wasn't anything going to go right?

It began to rain. Feeling miserable, she went to her room. She curled up in the hard, uncomfortable window-seat and peered outside. The thin drizzle seemed to be nagging at the dirty yellow leaves on the ash trees outside, telling them to hurry up and drop off.

Back in their old home at Lyme Regis you could enjoy the rain. It might mean a storm at sea was coming. Storms washed away the cliffs, and opened up whole new sites for fossil finds. Then you could go hunting for wonderful new discoveries.

Mama had often taken her on such adventures – hunting along the pebble banks and newly quarried rock faces for traces of Jurassic times! Then had come the long illness that had taken Mama away from them. Rose sighed as she watched the raindrops trickle slowly down the pane. Leaving the sea and the cliffs felt a bit like leaving her memories of Mama further behind.

She turned to her books again to escape her sad thoughts.

Later, Agatha called her down to lunch. Her father was too distracted to join her, so he sat in the drawing room, nervously nibbling the end of a fountain pen (something he told Rose never to do), and almost buried behind a pile of screwed-up paper.

"I'm composing a letter of complaint to that removal company," he explained. I'm threatening them with the law, unless they produce my missing chest immediately. Fearful shower of rogues!"

"Except we can't quite get it right," drawled her father's young assistant, Prendergast Ward. He was leaning his lanky frame against the mantelpiece, trying not to make it too obvious that he was hogging all the heat from the little fire in the grate.

"It's the detail," he agonised, pulling a pained face. "We would have 'ad it done ages ago, if it weren't for the blessed detail!"

Rose ate her vegetable broth in silence. Seeing Prendergast as large as life in the new house made her heart sink. She had rather hoped that, like Chest 13, he might have been lost in the move. He was supposed to be Papa's assistant, but whether he actually knew anything, or would ever be any help at all, remained to be seen.

The problem was that Prendergast was the nephew of the eccentric explorer Sir Lionel Mayhew. And Sir Lionel was the wealthy sponsor who gave Rose's father the funds to carry on with his work. Prendergast was an orphan and, with his uncle always off on some expedition or other, his education had been completely neglected. He had fallen into bad company at an early age, and was regarded – even by himself – as something of a good-for nothing. Now Sir Lionel was hoping to enter Prendergast into the great field of science – learning under Stanley Morrow's gentle guidance. Sir Lionel promised to keep giving Professor Morrow funds, as long as he found work for his lazy nephew. So the Morrows were rather stuck with Prendergast.

"I'll tell you what," said Stanley. "You need some recreation, Rose. Ever since we moved, you've been looking rather like a glum brontosaurus who's just been told the Ice Age is on its way." He forced a chuckle, trying to lighten the dismal atmosphere that had hung over them ever since they had arrived at their new house. He turned to Prendergast.

"While I'm clearing up in here, Mr Ward, why not take my daughter out for a stroll. You grew up in this great metropolis, didn't you?"

"I certainly did! Know it like the back of my 'and, I do."

"Well then – take command of an expedition. Why not treat her to some of the sights of London!"

"Yes, sir," barked out Prendergast, with a big toothy grin that made him look like a happy ape. "Just my idea, sir! That'll cheer 'er up! A Grand Tour, just the tonic she needs!"

Agatha smothered Rose in scarves, hat and cloak to prevent her getting a chill, and they set off, Prendergast whistling some tuneless music-hall song with great enthusiasm.

They had only just turned the corner at the side of their house when they saw an unusual sight. The street children – young beggars and ragamuffins who would run any message or carry any bag for a halfpenny or farthing – were playing around a stone statue. The bolder ones were diving between its legs and shouting out strange remarks.

"Bobby, bobby can't catch me!" sang one of the urchins, dancing round and round the figure.

Prendergast took a closer look at the statue and laughed. Rose was curious.

"What are they doing, Mr Ward?" she asked. Prendergast nosed a bit nearer, and the children backed away for a moment and fell silent.

"Oh, it's just a bit of fun. Look, someone's put a statue of a policeman in the road. These kids are having a lark with it. 'Bobby' is what they call a policeman, after that Bob Peel who started up this policing caper!"

Rose thought this very unusual.

"A statue of a policeman in our road? But there wasn't one yesterday."

"Well, there is now. What will they think of next? Very realistic it is, too!"

Rose went over to look at the statue. It was undoubtedly a policeman in uniform and, unlike most statues, which were rather big and grand, this one was exactly life-size. It wasn't on a plinth, either. It simply stood there in its stone boots on the roadside. The thing that struck Rose as really odd about it, however, was its face. Instead of the constable looking proud and dignified, his face wore an expression of fear and dread. The mouth hung open, and the stone eyes were staring out of their sockets as if they had seen a ghost.

What a funny way to carve a statue of a policeman, Rose thought. An icy shiver went down her back, but she wasn't really sure why.

CHAPTER FOUR

Prendergast had his own ideas about taking Rose on an interesting walk. He marched her along to the end of the street, where he found what he was looking for. Lurking under a dilapidated shop-awning was a scrawny youth with a feeble little moustache, and a habit of darting his eyes nervously from side to side.

"You stop 'ere and enjoy the view," Prendergast told her, gesturing vaguely at the empty road. "I'll just put a penny on Larky Larry in the three o'clock. Then we'll go 'ome, eh? The weather's as miserable as my granny."

The skinny youth was a 'runner', a lad who would take bets on horse races for you, then take your money to an illegal bookmaker at the race course. But Prendergast put more than a penny on his luck and Rose started to grow bored. Everyone knew that gambling went on all the time, and it wasn't exactly the crime of the century, but Rose still wasn't happy about being made a witness to Prendergast's rendezvous.

Freezing rain fell as Rose stood under the dripping shop-awning. She gazed up at the name of her new street. Headstone Lane. It sounded like the name of a graveyard.

As they wandered home, Rose simply couldn't get the strange and frightening events of the past two days out of her mind.

"Mr Ward," she ventured, "have you ever seen a funny man, all wrapped up in cloaks and scarves, standing around in our street? A very peculiar man who creeps along slowly like this…?" Bundled up in her own winter clothes, she gave a little theatrical imitation of the mystery figure.

Prendergast laughed. "Oh, you mean Mr Skellybones! Well done, Rose, that was just like 'im!"

"Mr Skellybones?" asked Rose, in surprise.

"That's what them street kids calls him. Apparently, if you ever catch a glimpse of his face, he looks all grey and bony – like an 'orrible old skellington."

Rose frowned. "Papa and I think he might be watching our house," she said. "We've seen him lurking about."

"Well, anyfing's possible," Prendergast replied. "But he's been seen about London for years. He's just some poor old geezer the kids laugh at. The way he creeps about, he must have the gout, lumbago and roomytism all mixed up together. Don't worry about 'im. He probably *will* be a skellybones before too long!" he chuckled.

Prendergast suddenly looked serious.

"But on the subject of watchin' the 'ouse… there's been some funny goings on, hasn't there!" he declared. "Robberies that aren't robberies, things moving in the night. It's a right old puzzle. The big mystery for me, is this missing chest. Your Papa's never told me much about it. Has he really lost something valuable? What's in it, exactly?"

"He doesn't know," answered Rose.

"Well, what's he worried about then? What you don't know can't 'urt you, as they say!"

"It's not like that," Rose tried to explain. "It's important because it's unknown. The point is, *nobody* will know what it is. It's something never seen on Earth before. If anyone knew what it was, then it wouldn't be so valuable."

Prendergast laughed. "Now you're talking science talk," he said. "Never could understand it. You're just like your Papa. Brilliant man, 'e is! Do you know 'e wrote eight letters saying sorry to the museum before you got up this mornin'? Throwed 'em all away though. It was the bloomin' detail you see… that's what bamboozled 'im…"

It made Rose sad to think of her father feeling nervous and writing letters to say he was sorry about things that weren't his fault. Nothing had really gone their way since they had arrived in London. She hoped he wouldn't be too miserable when they got home.

They were just approaching the house, when they spotted a pile of rubble on the pavement, with two street urchins looking at it. It was the policeman statue. Some-one had evidently knocked it over, and now it had shat-tered into pieces. Most of the children had run away in case they got in trouble for breaking it. Well, thought Rose, it had been a very odd place to put a statue. Whoever had put it there in the middle of the street had been very silly indeed.

"Shame about that," Prendergast suddenly remarked, pointing with his thumb at the stone debris. "Because it's just occurred to me, it was a very good likeness!"

"What do you mean?" asked Rose.

"Of one of the local bobbies I saw the other day. I thought there was something familiar about it when I saw it and now it's suddenly hit me. The statue was just like one of the regular bobbies I've seen pounding this beat. Odd that. It would've been funny to point it out to 'im!"

Rose felt a strange chill of horror. As they passed the stone constable, now in pieces, she turned her head away to avoid catching a glimpse of its awful staring eyes.

They were just climbing the steps to their front door, when suddenly an enormous man emerged from it, in a gigantic fur coat. Rose's father was showing him out, with utmost respect.

"Your hand, sir, your hand!" bellowed the stranger,

shaking hands with Professor Morrow for all he was worth. He fixed him with a shrewd eye, and clapped him on the back for good measure. "By Jupiter, sir! I just know we're going to be like brothers!"

Rose was astonished. She had never seen anyone be so friendly towards her father before. The huge gentleman was quite a spectacle, too, sporting a great moustache and bushy black beard. These, plus the monocle he wore, and his extraordinary Russian hat, gave him an air of faraway places and mysterious knowledge.

"Papa, Papa! Who was that?" Rose begged, as soon as he had gone. Professor Morrow patted all his pockets in a sort of panic, then pulled out a printed card and beamed happily.

"My dear Rose!" he said, "and my worthy Mr Ward, the most wonderful thing has happened. We are surely saved!"

"What is it?" asked Prendergast, open-mouthed. "'Oo was the geezer?"

"The gentleman," corrected Professor Morrow, "was none other than Hierophant Beelzebub, the great Fossil Collector and Grand Poobah of the International Dinosaur Club!"

He showed them the card proudly. "Do you know, that man has connections with the great University of Far-blaast in Siberia?"

"Look at this, and this –" He held up a sheaf of notes and leaflets all carrying the name and arms of the International Dinosaur Club.

"He gave me all of it! Hierophant has heard of my work and put me up to be a member! They have meetings and lectures, contacts and connections! Why, in one fell swoop, he can make me and my discoveries the talk of London! What a bit of luck!"

And to Rose's astonishment she saw her father dance a merry jig around the hall table.

"Strike a light!" cooed Prendergast. "He's gawn barmy!"

CHAPTER FIVE

There was something so curious about Mr Hierophant Beelzebub's leaflets that Rose took one upstairs with her to read that evening. She studied the letterhead. The crest in the centre showed a human skull and a grinning dinosaur skull, staring at each other, face to face. It was supposed to represent the new society Papa was so happy to be in. Rose found it creepy.

But when she climbed into bed, tiredness overcame her. With all sorts of extraordinary worries running through her mind, she drifted into a strange state, hardly knowing if she was asleep or awake.

In the dark it is always easy to imagine shapes and shadows moving around your room, but now Rose was imagining things in a way she never had before. She saw Mr Beelzebub's leaflets scattered on the bedside table, but in the queer glimmer of moonlight that peeked through her curtains, the pages seemed to be moving. It was as if tiny spiders were crawling all over them.

Then she realised that it wasn't spiders… it was the writing on the pamphlets! The words were coming to life and crawling off the pages. The inky squiggles joined together when they met up and made little pools of black slime that started to slurp down on to the floor and creep about, as if looking for something.

Gazing down in astonishment, Rose thought she could see tiny pointed stones appearing through the slime on the carpet. No, they weren't stones – they were cracked and broken bones – the tips of terrible claws rising up through the floor!

Rose's scientific mind refused to believe it. She screwed her eyes shut and looked again.

Nothing. She let out a sigh of relief – the claws and the slime had gone. How could her mind play such tricks? Was the London smog giving her hallucinations?

Suddenly the darkness exploded with light. For an instant the room was lit by a flash of fire. Rose screamed, and all around her the darkness seemed to echo with answering cries.

Terrified, she covered her ears, but the screams didn't go away. Instead they all joined together, into one great awful screech, the like of which she had never heard before.

Rose held her breath as strange visions stirred in the night once more. The creaking joints of huge wings unfurled to stretch across the room. Suddenly, colossal jaws with rows of sharp teeth snapped up at her from the darkness. She realised she was staring into the mouth of a huge flying lizard.

Another flash of lightning lit the room, and the prehistoric phantom popped like a soap bubble and vanished.

She gasped. Was the house haunted? By dinosaurs? She waited and waited in an agony of suspense, but the strange visions had disappeared. But now she could hear thumping and knocking noises in the study below.

Under a kind of spell, not knowing what was real or unreal, Rose crept downstairs. She had to know what was going on! Her father had always taught her there was a sensible explanation for everything, and she kept telling herself that now. As Rose crept towards the study door, the thumping grew louder. And now she could hear other sounds, strange creakings and scrapings. Suddenly a hand grabbed her shoulder.

"Oh, Miss Morrow! Let me go in first!" hissed Agatha, pale and scared under her nightcap. "There's probably a cat got in through the winder. More than one from the sounds of it – I can here 'em rummaging about!"

Rose felt much better seeing Agatha there, carrying an umbrella in her hand to use in case of emergency. But as she slowly turned the handle of the door, and the strange noises carried on, Rose held her breath.

Crash! There was a clattering from all corners of the room as the door flew open and they looked inside. In the dim moonlight they could hardly see a thing.

"Shoo! Shoo!" cried out Agatha, as she stepped boldly into the room, waving her umbrella. She tripped over something on the floor and went flying. Rose fell over her and stumbled right into the middle of the room. Something flew into her face and scratched her cheek. Rose screamed, and flapped wildly with her hand, hitting something soft and furry, and sending it squealing across the room.

"A bat! A bat!" screeched Agatha. "Open the door and let it out!"

Rose fumbled in the dark, grabbed the nearest door handle, and tugged at it. It was locked. Agatha sprang to her side, and turned the key. Rose screamed again as she felt something collide crazily into the back of her head and get tangled in her hair. As the door shot open, she ran outside, desperate to get free from whatever it was. She screamed and ran blindly out into the night, with no idea of where she was going.

CHAPTER SIX

Wings still beat madly above her as she darted down the passage trying to shake off her pursuer. Deeper and deeper she ran into the maze of alleys behind the house, an evil-smelling labyrinth of hidden ways and dead ends, piled with rubbish.

In desperation she dived under a dark archway into pitch blackness. She felt rotten wood splinter under her, and the ground disappeared beneath her feet.

She fell with a thump on to a stone ledge just a few feet beneath her, then tumbled down some steps, landing in a heap at the bottom. She lay there panting, and feeling bruised all over. All was still. The only thing she could hear was her own breathing.

"I've done it!" she thought. "I've shaken them off!"

As the moon came out from behind a cloud, Rose had just enough light to see rows of bottles, decked with cobwebs, and rotting piles of empty, split old barrels. It was damp, and fungus seemed to be crawling everywhere, giving off a faint sickly glimmer in the moonlight.

She realised she had fallen through into an abandoned cellar. Now that the bats had gone, Rose's common sense flooded back, and she was furious with herself for rushing away from the safety of home.

She was just beginning to crawl painfully up the steps when she heard something that made her freeze. Two distant muttering voices were gradually getting closer. She stayed as silent as possible.

Straining to hear, Rose could make out two speakers. One had a thin, cracked voice, and sounded like a sulky child. The other spoke with a cold, distant whisper, which made a nasty gurgling sound every time it breathed in.

"It isn't there! It isn't there!" cried Squeaky.

"Silence!" hissed Gurgly. "Don't speak of it! "

"And we nearly got caught! We made one of them run for its life – but I'm sure it didn't see us clearly! Anyway, we're going back home," said the first voice, sounding angry. "Why take these chances now? We can't let the Dwimolum – the day-crawlers – discover us, when their downfall is so close!"

"I must be sure. The pieces are so nearly in place. I can feel it. Their presence is so strong here, it calls out to me. I'm sure I felt magic working here tonight. Ancient, deep magic!"

"Ahk!" squealed the first voice, with wicked delight.

"Soon *she* will come, and then everything will change! Then the cursed surface-vermin, the light-makers, will bow down in fear!"

"Fear? These Dwimolum have forgotten how to be afraid. But soon the Great Fear will return, and with it the Realm That Was! Our day is close at hand. Flee then, back to your skulking holes. I have no more commands for you tonight!"

The two voices became fainter, then disappeared. Rose rubbed her head, too dazed and frightened to guess what the bizarre conversation had been about.

A soft beam of moonlight seemed to invite her up the steps. Slowly, Rose emerged from the cellar, and peeped cautiously out of the rotten trapdoor. The coast was clear. Moving as quietly as she could, she followed the path where the light led her most brightly.

Moments later, she stepped into a beautiful little garden. It was overgrown with great bearded creepers of ancient ivy. Strange stone monuments were half-hidden under drifts of withered leaves. Hanging plants with long curling tendrils spilled from hollows in crumbling stone walls. The air seemed rich with memories of distant ages. Rose felt she had stumbled into a place of enchantment.

In the centre was a small stone angel. It was about half as tall as Rose, with stone wings folded down its back. The statue's face was turned towards her, with a calm expression of distant peace. Rose stepped closer to it, somehow feeling it would protect her.

The little angel was so finely cut, so delicately portrayed that Rose gazed at it in wonder. All her worries and fears of the night were washed away in its calm presence. Then she saw that in the palm of its right hand, held out towards her, was a white stone, shaped like a crescent moon.

Rose had the oddest feeling that it was being offered to her, that she must take it.

"It might bring me good luck," she said to herself, as she clutched it tightly.

Then suddenly it was as if a spell had been broken. The moonlight was cut off by a great dark cloud – or was it a cloud? As Rose glanced up, she had the extraordinary impression that the moon was being blotted out by an immense flock of bats. The wondrous garden fell into shadow, and somewhere far away Agatha was screaming for her to come back.

CHAPTER SEVEN

"We've 'ad more than bats in 'ere!" declared Cook, glaring around the study in morning's first light. Stanley Morrow was distraught. This time, instead of the bizarre tampering with cases and bones he had discovered before, there was clear evidence of a thorough search – everything had been opened up, pried into, then tossed aside. He was tying his hanky in knots in dismay.

"It was very, very foolish of you, Agatha, to come investigating the disturbance on your own. Very brave, but quite, quite wrong! And as for you, Rose…" Her father dried up, lost for words.

He began to usher them out of the room. "It's quite obvious to me now that we are beset by a most dastardly gang of burglars. You must have disturbed them before they could take anything. As for cats and bats and what-not, the thieves must have left the back door open, and half the local wildlife found its way in here out of the cold. Now I must report this to the police!"

When Professor Morrow returned from the police station, he was surprised to find a messenger from the International Dinosaur Club waiting for him in the hall.

"Mr Hierophant Beelzebub begs to forgive the intrusion on your time, sir," the messenger said. He was a boy of about ten, putting on the most formal and impressive display of haughtiness he could muster. "But you are falling behind on your payments to the International Dinosaur Club!"

Professor Morrow was a little flustered. "There must be some mistake!" he replied. "Why, I haven't even joined the club yet!"

"Mr Beelzebub begs me to inform you that in receiving his leaflets yesterday, you are considered to have joined already, in which case, he will require a small fee of five pounds – this fee to be paid by return messenger."

"Five pounds? That's rather a lot!" Professor Morrow sighed. He fluttered about and mumbled and dithered a while, then went to his desk and made out a cheque for the whole amount, which he carefully signed and put into an envelope for the messenger to return.

"It does seem like a lot," he said to no one in particular, as he sat thoughtfully at his desk. "But it's a small price to pay for the services of such an excellent fellow as Hierophant. I'm sure he'll be just the man to help track down my missing Chest 13!"

Rose had decided not to tell her father about her bizarre visions of the night before. Poor Papa had more than enough things on his mind. Until Rose was quite sure of what had really happened, she would keep quiet. If she mentioned the phantom dinosaur in her room, Papa would probably think she was going mad. He would certainly think she was becoming too obsessed with pre-historic creatures. He might even ban her from studying her beloved fossils!

Agatha and Cook mollycoddled her all morning, after her scare. She was being treated for the scratch she received, Agatha having her own mixtures for such things, passed down from her grandmother.

Her father didn't really like her spending too much time with the servants, but the cosy basement kitchen was the only truly warm and inviting place in the house, and Rose loved being allowed down there. Now she had an excuse to sit near the oven, and enjoy the smells of cook-ing – Cook was preparing a plum pudding – while she was being nursed by Agatha.

"We can't be too careful," Agatha said. "Who knows what it was that scratched your pretty face. A good job last night wasn't All Hallows Eve – or I would've sworn it was one of them things that go bump in the night!"

"Oh, Aggie, don't go scaring Miss Rosemary. She's much too full of science to believe your nonsense!" said

Cook.

"All I know is what I saw was much too big to be a bat... a normal sort of bat, anyway!" Agatha replied.

Cook went quiet. Rose looked at her face in the mirror. Agatha's nursing had made the cut sting quite badly. She touched the moon-shaped stone in her pocket, and it seemed to make her feel better. As she held it, in her mind's eye she could see the kind face of the stone angel looking peacefully back at her. What had really happened last night? Rose wondered if she was right to keep all her adventures to herself.

"Do you know anything about that old garden, some-where behind the house?" Rose ventured. "I saw it when I got lost in the alleyways last night. It was so beautiful in the moonlight!"

"Oh, yes," Agatha replied. "Sweet little place, isn't it? They call it the Memorial Garden around here, I'm told, but what it's remembering of, I don't know!"

Rose was about to ask about the little angel, when Cook suddenly loomed over both of them, in a rather conspiratorial way. Rose and Agatha looked up at her in surprise.

"Now," said Cook in a hushed voice, rubbing some flour off her hands. "It's funny what you should say, about seein' something much too big to be a bat." She stopped and looked behind her carefully. "Very funny indeed."

"Why?" asked Rose. "Whatever do you mean?"

"Well," Cook said slowly. "Last year, my 'usband, Joe, and a few 'undred others, 'ad jobs workin' on the diggin's for the new underground railway line they're makin'. And 'e told me 'e saw things down there that ain't never been seen in any zoo – or ever been told about in any newspaper."

Her voice became quieter and Rose and Agatha huddled closer to listen.

"Great 'airy bats there were! Enormous creatures. But with the 'eads and tails of rats. And they was full of mischief, always knockin' over lamps and stealin' things – like naughty children! The men didn't know whether they was rats or bats, so they used to call 'em 'brats'!"

"Don't listen, Miss Rose!" Agatha hissed, but by now both she and Rose were all ears, and Cook was in no mood to stop.

"But the thing that really gave my Joe the willies," she carried on, "was their eyes. 'E said they weren't blind bats – they 'ad a sort of look in their eyes, as if they was workin' things out, and thinkin' up thoughts. Almost as if they was as clever as you and me! Joe even reckoned 'e 'eard 'em chatterin' away to each other, in a funny kind of language.

"Some of the men started to get the creeps and they

wouldn't work down there if there was brats about. So one night, the boss sent six rat-catchers down. Real crafty lads they were – they knew all the tricks, puttin' down arsenic and huntin' with dogs and ferrets."

Cook's voice sank to a tiny whisper.

"'Ow many of them lads do you think was ever seen again?"

Rose and Agatha held their breath, and waited for the answer.

"Only one!" Cook whispered. "An' 'e 'ad completely lost 'is wits. The workmen found 'im in the mornin' at the end of a tunnel, all starin'-eyed and lookin' like 'e'd been dragged through a forest of thorns backwards. No one could ever make 'im talk about what 'appened. And they say that lad 'as never caught another rat again, or done 'arm to any livin' thing. Just the sight of a bat makes 'im go barmy now!

"After the disappearin' rat-catchers, none of the men would go near the brats. That's why some of the deeper diggin' was called off, not for the reasons they give in the papers like cave-ins and floodin'. But in the main tunnels the nasty creatures sort of moved out anyway after a while, without bein' asked. Joe says they disappeared down deeper into the sewers, after proper lights was put in. It was the lights what scared 'em away, 'e reckoned!"

Usually Rose laughed at Cook's stories, but something

about this one made her very uneasy. It was bad enough to bump into bats in the dead of night at all, without people making it worse. She wandered through the house, lost in strange doubts. There is a scientific explanation for everything, Rose told herself. Absolutely everything. She stood in the back garden, her eyes filling with tears because of the cold wind.

The scientific explanation could be that I'm going mad.

CHAPTER EIGHT

Standing in the dismal chill of the back garden, Rose listed everything to herself, to try to understand the strange things that had happened since she came to London. Making lists, looking at facts squarely, was the scientific method. That was what she believed in – science and sense, not silly stories! There had to be a way to understand what was happening, and she would find it.

This was the list that she thought out to herself:

1. Father's thirteenth chest goes missing, with an important part of Skeleton X in it.
2. Strange man watches our house, Mr Skellybones.
3. Thieves turn study upside-down, and play a prank with dinosaur bones. Papa calls police.
4. Stone statue of constable appears in our street.
5. Phantom dinosaurs in my room.
6. Attacked by bat.
7. Hear strangest conversation in middle of night about

surface people having to fear something terrible.

8. Discover magic garden and pick up lucky moonstone…

The list rapidly grew so long that it made Rose feel more, rather than less, baffled.

Clonk! The noise made Rose jump, but it was only the sound of someone in the garden next door.

"Clip clop, clip clop, giddy up, Horsie!" came a girl's sing-song voice. Rose broke out of her maze of thoughts, once again hoping to find a friend amid her troubles.

"Hello, there!" she called. "How do you do? I'm sorry we haven't been properly introduced…"

All went silent behind the wall.

"I was so silly when I told you I hadn't got any friends. I'm not surprised you thought I was horrid," Rose began. She had been planning this speech for a day or two. "Really I have lots of them, only not here. Not in London."

There was a scraping noise next door, which Rose guessed was the sound of a wooden 'horsie' being turned around. Then the silence was broken.

"Mama says I was very wrong to speak to you like I did," began the voice in a quiet tone. Rose was very pleased to hear this – it was better than she had expected and sounded rather apologetic.

"Oh, don't worry about that!" Rose said. "I'm sure it's most unpleasant to be shouted at over a wall, and I –"

"Mama says I shouldn't speak to you *at all*!" the voice screeched. Rose's heart sank as she heard Horsie galloping back indoors.

Going inside herself, she wanted to rush back to her room and lose herself in her books when she saw her father in the hallway. He was standing there spluttering and rubbing his tired eyes, as he often did when he was feeling harassed.

"Well, this is most unusual!" he was muttering. "I've just had to pay a shilling apiece for the leaflets and documents about the International Dinosaur Club – I was quite sure that Hierophant gave them to me free. Why, I've been fending off messengers half the morning!"

Prendergast strolled in from the drawing room.

"You should welcome them, one and all," he said. "Pay up and pay gladly, Professor Morrow. That club is the best fing that ever 'appened to you!"

Just then there was a ring on the bell. Another messenger appeared, bowing and scraping in the hallway, asking to speak to Sir Stanley Morrow, on a matter of some urgency.

"I'm not 'Sir' Stanley," Professor Morrow corrected him impatiently. But the messenger, a thin gentleman in a dark suit and cloak, with a top hat under his arm, was already reading aloud from a sheet of paper in his hand.

"The International Dinosaur Club regrets to inform you that you are three days late with your annual membership fee. Please send a cheque for five English pounds by return messenger."

"Another five pounds! Why, that is a small fortune!" gasped Professor Morrow. "I've paid more than enough already, there must be some mistake. I'll speak to Mr Beelzebub personally…" He opened the front door and gestured the visitor towards the steps. But the messenger would not budge.

"Begging your pardon, your eminence. You have already paid a five-pound entrance fee to join the society, agreed. But this new payment is for this year's membership. Surely, sir, you can't join the club and then not want to be a member!"

"But I thought joining made me a member!"

"Oh no, sir. Societies aren't that simple."

By now Stanley had become annoyed. "I shan't pay anyway, until I speak to Mr Beelzebub again. Good day."

It was as if a cloud suddenly passed over their visitor. Instead of being polite and fawning, he seemed to writhe in his cloak like an angry serpent.

"If you do not pay… you will be cast out!" he declared. Then, with a fiery look, he turned and vanished into the bustling street.

"Extraordinary business! Why, the cheek of these people!" said Stanley, closing the door. "And what a peculiar person!"

He sat at his desk and sipped a cup of lemon tea that Agatha had brought. Rose felt sorry for him. Meeting Mr Beelzebub had been the only thing that had cheered her father up recently. Now this Dinosaur Club business was turning into a worry as well.

"Ah, that's better," Stanley said, enjoying his tea. "I just want life to get back to normal for a while."

It was then that the police arrived. Within moments Rose's father had put on his coat and had been whisked away into the gloomy winter afternoon, on the trail of the missing chest.

CHAPTER NINE

It was evening before Rose's father returned. For an instant, before he could say anything, Rose thought how wonderful it would be if he brought good news, and all their troubles were over.

But he threw himself down in a chair, and cried out, "Hopeless! Completely hopeless!"

"What 'appened?" asked Prendergast anxiously. "The er, bobbies, gone 'ave they?" He looked about keenly.

"Yes, for what they were worth!" groaned Professor Morrow.

He allowed Agatha to pour him a glass of whisky – and he sipped it slowly, looking more like an invalid than a man who had been on an adventure.

"The police finally managed to track down the 'Better Safe Than Sorry' removal company," he began. "They had been most elusive – it seems they had removed their head office to a new location."

"Not that unusual – for a removal company," pointed

out Prendergast helpfully. Professor Morrow ignored him.

"After some pretty stiff talk from the Inspector, they managed to dig up a Book of Works, supposedly documenting their every job, and filled with the most awful scrawl you can imagine.

"Now, one entry in this book stated that my chest had been mislaid for a day or two, but was then delivered here. The book actually stated, 'Chest handed over to Mr Morrow in person'! Can you believe the cheek of these people? 'In person' my foot!"

"Sounds like a pack of lies!" said Prendergast. "You can't trust none of these removalling types. Bunch of villains, the lot of 'em!"

"That may well be the case," Stanley agreed. "But we shall probably never know. Because the lad who made the delivery has disappeared."

"Disappeared?" asked Rose.

"They say he left on a merchant ship for East India yesterday! By now he could be anywhere. My only clue, my only contact with my lost chest, has vanished! So then the police said they had done about all they could do to help me. They even asked me if I was one of these 'forgetful professors' and maybe I did have the chest somewhere at home after all!"

"Ridiculous!" chimed in Prendergast. "Downright

liberty!"

"When I reminded them about the series of burglaries we've had here, in which nothing was taken, they looked at me as if I was completely raving. The Inspector even said that he'd sent a constable down the other night to keep a watch on our house, and he hadn't been seen since! He looked at me as if that was my fault!"

At this remark, Rose shivered. A disappearing constable? And a stone statue of a policeman turning up in their street! She drove her strange fears into the darkest corner of her mind.

"All in all, it's been a very sorry affair. I'm afraid I really don't know what to do now," sighed Professor Morrow. "After all this, the trail is a hopeless dead end!"

It certainly seemed to be. But one good thing had come out of their day of shocks. Rose's father was now completely convinced that after three fruitless searches the thieves would finally leave their house alone.

And it seemed that he was right. The next day dawned without a single drama of any kind. The study was undisturbed and Rose had no weird visions or dreams. But this didn't surprise her too much. She had slept with her lucky moonstone under her pillow and she was sure it was protecting her.

Professor Morrow ordered that long faces were to be banned from the house and even gave Prendergast the money to take Rose out for a special lunch as a treat, while he started to put his affairs back into order.

Prendergast's idea of a treat was to take Rose to WF Gipple's Pie and Mash shop in Old Brompton Road.

"They'll do you a corking feed 'ere!" he announced, his eyes lighting up as they reached the grimy little eating house. Inside it was pandemonium. Customers were shouting for attention and the serving girls were yelling at each other. Everyone was telling everyone else to hurry up with something, and the clatter of pots and pans from the kitchen added to the din. Steam was rising up from great metal tubs and a distinct smell of burning filled the air. Rose watched in a kind of fascinated horror, as the girl behind the counter smeared a dollop of mash on to a man's plate, upturned two charred pies next to it – the black pastry shattering in all directions – then dribbled a mysterious green liquor on top.

"Luvverly!" grinned Prendergast, watching the performance. "Same again, twice!" He grinned at the girl. She was a hard-faced young woman who looked as if she had never smiled in her life. Her hands were red and raw. Rose guessed the poor girl must spend half her life peeling endless potatoes to fill the gigantic drum of steaming mash.

They couldn't find a place to sit at on their own, so Prendergast jammed himself in on the end of a table, where an old woman in a shabby shawl and bonnet was feeding three noisy children on plates of bony eel in glistening jelly.

There was a sudden "yipe!" as Prendergast stepped on the tail of a dog that was curled up under the table. It didn't bother Prendergast a bit, and while the children started to fuss over their "poor doggie", he just laughed and said, "That'll learn 'im!"

Rose gazed at her giant meal in dismay. It was about six times more than she could possibly eat. Under the crust of her pie was a mysterious grey sloshy substance. She was frightened to ask what it was. All anyone ever asked for was "pie" – no one seemed to know or care what kind of pie it was.

"Talking about your Papa," Prendergast suddenly blurted out, although they hadn't even mentioned him since leaving the house. "He's the cleverest man I've ever met. Much cleverer than my Uncle Lionel even, who's a bit of a silly old duffer, between you and me."

He thrust a great forkful of pie into his huge mouth and chewed it thoughtfully. Rose had found to her surprise that the green liquid was quite nice in a funny sort of way, and with the mash it was certainly warm and filling.

"But," Prendergast continued, with his mouth full, "I would say it wasn't up to his usual cleverness, gettin' involved with the police. Now that is a very chancey business. They'll up and stick you in jail for next to nothink these days. They're a law unto themselves!"

Rose thought this was funny. "But they are the law, surely Mr Ward?" Prendergast frowned deeply, and suddenly pitched his voice very low.

"They say the law 'as a long arm, Rosemary," said Prendergast, "but it also 'as a very long nose. Best to keep away from that nose, that's all I'm saying. If your father should show any sign of taking up detective work again, and should he ask your advice – because he does pay a deal of attention to what you tell 'im – just warn him off draggin' the flippin' bobbies into it. That's all I'm saying. They leave no detail unturned. And it's the detail what'll do you, every time!" he concluded.

Rose finished her meal in silence. Why was Prendergast so worried about the police all of a sudden? Was there more to him than met the eye?

CHAPTER TEN

Agatha opened the door and in came the enormous figure of Hierophant Beelzebub. He was followed by three mysterious gentlemen, bundled up in great coats, their faces half-hidden by mufflers, with big furry hats pulled down almost over their eyes. Their unusual garb was completed by the big woolly mittens they all wore.

"My friend, my dear friend!" beamed Mr Beelzebub, shaking Stanley Morrow vigorously by the hand. "What a great day this is for science!"

"It is?" said Professor Morrow, quite taken aback. He had spent a long, tiring day putting his study back in order, and this cheerful tone from Hierophant was most welcome. He had half-expected an awkward scene about all the cash demands made by the International Dinosaur Club.

"Yes, of course. For tonight is the night you join The Great Collection!"

Professor Morrow looked puzzled. He was very

pleased to find Hierophant in a warm, genial mood, but was rather uncomfortable at the presence of the three bundled-up gentlemen. While Hierophant was talking to him, they were shuffling around the room picking up any fossils or curios they could find, holding them in their mittens and muttering between themselves in an unintelligible foreign language.

Rose thought their behaviour incredibly rude. She had been studying a book about rocks, trying to find out exactly what her moonstone was made from. Now she just glared over the book at the invaders.

"What's The Great Collection?" asked Professor Morrow, intrigued.

Mr Beelzebub wrapped an arm around Professor Morrow's shoulder. His teeth glittered in a big tigerish grin beneath his great black moustache. "A wonderful idea – a grand design – a golden vision!" he declared. "The International Dinosaur Club inspects and documents all the finds and discoveries of its members. We gather together all the greatest items to make a great treasury of knowledge!"

Professor Morrow looked slightly uncertain. "You gather them together?" he asked in a quiet voice.

"Why yes! We search your collection for its greatest finds, list them, gather them and, in short, sir, we take them. At no charge to yourself!"

Smash! Professor Morrow jumped, as one of the odd men knocked over a vase, while trying to remove a dried bullrush from it with his big clumsy mittens.

"Smash a vase and win a prize!" said Prendergast sarcastically. "What do you think you're playing at? Come on, Professor Morrow, get him to call 'em off!"

The men all turned at once and faced Prendergast. They started shuffling towards him in a curious way, stretching out their mittened hands, like sleepwalkers.

"'Ere, what's goin' on?" Prendergast said, backing away.

"Cancalibour!" shouted Mr Beelzebub in a commanding voice, which reminded Rose of a stage magician saying "Abracadabra". The men stopped in their tracks and turned to face him.

"Come through to the study! Let The Great Collection commence!" Mr Beelzebub muttered some other outlandish words and the shuffling figures forgot Prendergast and made for the doorway to the hall.

"I say, I say!" stammered Professor Morrow, dashing to the door and blocking their path. "This is really most irregular!"

The men turned and faced Mr Beelzebub, making quizzical noises. It was a distinctly peculiar performance and something about it was giving Rose the creeps.

"Now, let us discuss the matter, my good Mr

Beelzebub," said Professor Morrow. "A collector's finds are his personal treasure, his only security! I don't understand this idea of yours of simply taking them away. Taking them where? For how long?"

"All that will be explained in future Dinosaur Club newsletters. Now come along my good fellow. As a member of our club you simply must be part of The Great Collection. You've signed! You're in! There's no choice in the matter!"

"I certainly do have a choice!" Professor Morrow objected. "Besides, your constant stream of messengers assure me I am not a proper member!"

Mr Beelzebub suddenly narrowed his eyes, in a thoughtful scowl. "Why yes," he said with a low, humourless laugh, "you do owe us certain monies and assurances. We must certainly begin collecting items to cover your debt to the club! Onward, my Collectors!"

Suddenly the men pressed forward and barged through the door. Professor Morrow had to get out of their way pretty quickly to avoid being knocked down.

"Get out!" he shouted. "Get out or I'll call the police!"

Professor Morrow grabbed at one of the men and a big mitten came off in his hand. Rose's father stared.

"Good heavens... your... your hand!" he stuttered. Where a hand should have been, there was a pale stunted claw. It looked withered, almost skeleton-like. Two sets of fingers were somehow stuck together, as if they had grown into each other. A cold air seemed to fill the passageway. The men turned towards Professor Morrow and began to surround him. He backed away, turning white with fright, as they bore down on him.

"Cancalibour!"

Rose had shouted the word almost without knowing what she was doing. But it had worked for Mr Beelzebub, and it worked for her. The Collectors stopped, and turned to face her. Then they saw something that made them freeze, and let out a low moaning sound.

When Rose had leaped up to shout, she had knocked her book over, revealing something which had been lying on the desk behind it – the moonstone. The men stared at it and started to back away. They began to wail pathetically. Then, almost falling over each other, they made a dash for the front door.

"Come back, come back, you fools!" cried Hierophant Beelzebub, following them out into the street. Stanley slammed the door behind them and secured every bolt and chain with lightning speed.

Suddenly, the bizarre invasion was over. When he was absolutely sure they had no intention of returning, Professor Morrow told Prendergast to stay at home, while he reported everything to the police.

In all the confusion, it hadn't really been obvious to

anyone except Rose why the frightened men had run away. Her father simply thought he was dealing with a bunch of raving madmen. But Rose knew differently. She held the stone in the palm of her hand, and silently thanked it for its help. Again she seemed to see the gentle, kind-faced angel in her mind. She had so many questions in her head, and it became clear to her that there was one place where she might get some answers.

When the fuss had died down, Rose slipped out through the study door. Clutching her lucky stone tightly, she made her way through the maze of alleys, to find the Memorial Garden. She remembered how enchanted it had seemed, like a perfectly safe place in which nothing could go wrong. That was where she needed to be now, to try to understand all the strange things happening around her.

Then came the shock. She found the garden, but everything had changed. Her magical place looked dull, small, lifeless somehow. The trees that had seemed so beautiful in the moonlight were just drab, ordinary little things. The stone monuments were less impressive than she remembered them.

And most surprising of all, the stone angel had completely disappeared.

CHAPTER ELEVEN

People can only be scared for so long, before something inside them snaps, and they decide they have to do something about it. Rose was starting to feel like this. Since leaving her nice home by the sea, she had been beset by horrid creatures, odd people and strange hauntings. Now, the morning after the invasion of the Collectors, her mind full of mysteries, and her friendly stone angel having vanished, she felt she had reached a turning point.

Saying that mysterious word yesterday had given her a strange sense of power and command. Cancalibour, she said to herself comfortingly, wondering what it could mean. Her father had praised her for her quick thinking. Obviously the foreign word had meant a lot to the bizarre Collectors. But why had the stone frightened them so?

"There's something going on," Rose told herself, as she went downstairs. "Something to do with bats and burglaries and stolen statues and Mr Hierophant Beelzebub! But one thing's for sure. I'm not going to be frightened any more!"

Prendergast was reading his *Sporting Journal* as usual. He gave Rose a miserable look.

"As if all these Mitten Men wasn't bad enough, Rosemary, you didn't bring me any luck on them gee-gees. They all lost, every one!" He eyed her gloomily, as if it was her fault for being with him when he had placed his bets.

"Just get rid of it, can't you?" Professor Morrow's voice was coming from the passageway, where he was giving Agatha rather a hard time.

"There's a horrid smell in this hall – like being underground." He sniffed the air again quizzically. "Lime! That's what it smells like. Where it came from I don't know."

"What about the horrid men, Papa?" Rose asked. "Who were they?"

"The Collectors?" Professor Morrow said. "I am sure that one of them must be suffering from a terrible wasting disease. Did you see his hand? But the whole business is too peculiar for words!" I must find out more about Mr Beelzebub, and I think I know where to go!"

The Natural History Museum loomed up before them, dark and dreary in the grim, lightless London morning. Rose gazed at the stonework, the carved shapes of long-extinct birds and ancient reptiles peering down at her. Hundreds of tall windows revealed glimpses of endless rooms and corridors full of secrets, and of unknown men studying unknown things in silent offices.

"Someone here will have to know about this wretched Dinosaur Club!" Professor Morrow said, as they approached the broad steps to the main entrance. "I won't go away until someone speaks to me!"

They waited in the hall while a clerk ran off to fetch some other higher-up clerk, who might be able to speak to the assistant of one of the secretaries. It was all very frustrating. As they waited in the chilly hallway, a workman came and left a box of pointed stones just inside the door.

"Fossil teeth, from a sabre-toothed tiger, I should imagine," Rose's father muttered vaguely. He was too preoccupied with his anger at being made to stay outside and wait to show his usual interest.

"Fossil teeth, are they?" asked a croaky voice from behind them. They turned, and saw a bent little old man facing them. He had a pale, slightly ill look about him; his bright yellow neckerchief was the only touch of colour in an otherwise sombre suit.

"And what would you know about such things?" the old man asked. He had the face of a starved bird, with a long beaky, enquiring nose, and rather odd, bulging eyes.

"Oh, absolutely nothing – in London, it seems!" replied Professor Morrow. "Here I am just a target for any robber or madman, or else I'm just a novice student to be ignored and put off by servants. However, before I came to this city it seemed I was quite an expert in my field."

Rose's father was feeling very distressed, and it brought out a bitter side to him.

"Now that is interesting..." the old man said. "Would it surprise you to know that I am Professor Morris Lillian, the Museum's Chief Curator of Fossils?" He reached into his bag. "Just tell me what you know about this fine specimen of a cervical vertebra from an iguanodon. I'll be back in a moment – I seem to have mislaid my hat..." And he pottered off to find it.

Professor Morrow was thrilled. "Professor Lillian! One of the greatest fossil men in the land! What a privilege! Why, the things I must ask him!"

Rose's father was too excited even to look closely at the fossil in his hand. "I must get off on the right foot with him. I'll tell him his cervical vertebra is the finest specimen ever!"

But Rose looked closely at the bone her father held. She frowned, and then looked anxious.

"Papa! I... I do believe that isn't a cervical vertebra at all!"

"Now don't witter, dear! I must work out what to say to him!" Stanley replied.

"But look – it's part of a tailbone from a megalosaurus.

I was copying one out of a book at home only last week. I'd know it anywhere!"

Professor Morrow stared at the fossil. "Is... is it possible that the greatest expert in the land can be wrong?" he asked. Now that Rose had pointed it out, he realised how right she was.

"Good heavens!" gasped Professor Morrow. "Am I to disagree with Professor Lillian?"

Just then the professor returned, smiling broadly. "What do you think then, sir? Finest example you've ever seen, what?"

"It's a very fine specimen, indeed, sir," agreed Stanley. He gulped. He had decided he must be true to his scientific principles. He took a deep breath, then told Professor Lillian he was wrong.

CHAPTER TWELVE

"Well done, well done!" cackled the old professor. "There are so many frauds and bogus experts in our profession that I like to set that little trap for them. It takes a lot of character to disagree with a Chief Curator of Fossils! Now, you must introduce yourself… "

As soon as Lillian heard Professor Morrow's name, he shook his hand firmly and said how much he admired his work. He said he had been so disappointed that Professor Morrow's lecture, 'The Impossible Dinosaur', had been postponed. When he heard about the missing chest he was full of sympathy. Rose's father was absolutely delighted. Forgetting all about the International Dinosaur Club, he followed Lillian, as the curious old man showed him one fascinating exhibit after another.

"What a stroke of luck, meeting you Professor Morrow," Morris Lillian said. "I'm just putting together a team of experts to help with my new Iguanodon Gallery. You must come on board! There is an enormous amount of work to do. You'll be paid a first-class rate, I can assure you!"

Professor Morrow could hardly believe his luck. They were led through a door into a corridor not open to the public, and Professor Lillian took them into his own private chambers and gave them elevenses. Rose's father drank the finest Darjeeling tea, while Rose was treated to Lillian's special tin of shortbread biscuits. It seemed to her she had never tasted anything so delicious.

Best of all was what happened next. Professor Lillian went to see Sir Gordon Bowler to tell him how useful Professor Morrow would be to them. Before Rose's father knew it, he was shaking hands with Sir Gordon and being welcomed aboard. Sir Gordon didn't mention his disappointment over the missing chest at all. He even made a joke out of it.

"It seems your 'Impossible Dinosaur' is going to be even more impossible to produce than you realised!" he chuckled. Everyone laughed, although Rose didn't really think it was funny. Sir Gordon called Professor Morrow 'my esteemed colleague' and said he was looking forward to working with him. Stanley Morrow was too happy to speak. He had much to learn about his new job, but he took Rose home first and let her spread the good news.

Rose was so proud of her father. Seeing him take tea in the rooms of the Chief Curator of Fossils had made her feel that he had really arrived. He was about to become a famous scientist, as she had always hoped and dreamed.

Agatha was thrilled when she heard the news.

"Ooh, we'll be rich now, and Professor Morrow will be able to hire me a little undermaid to boss around!" she laughed. Cook immediately started giving herself airs and graces.

"This isn't just good news for Professor Morrow – it makes the whole household more important! Just think – me, personal cook to a famous professor!"

"Now Rosie," said Agatha, "you must run along and tell Mr Ward the news. He needs cheerin' up, he's been mooning around that miserable today…"

Rose went out of the side door and then across a small courtyard to the little neighbouring cottage where Prendergast's rooms were. The dwelling had been built originally to house extra servants, but proved perfect for Stanley to lodge his assistant without having to put up with him all hours of the day and night.

Rose tapped on the door, but there was no reply. She called his name loudly, but there was no answer. She thought he might possibly be dozing and unable to hear her.

The door was ajar, and Rose was curious to see inside. She tiptoed through the hall, and peered through the door into his quarters. He wasn't at home. But his room was such an indescribable mess, Rose could not help having a look around.

There was a jumble of coats and cloaks, hung up just about anywhere except in the wardrobe, and a pile of hats perched on a human skull he had collected from somewhere. There was a weird assortment of African masks, spears, tom-toms and other strange foreign artifacts (probably presents from his uncle), and books on all sorts of subjects he was supposed to be studying (but didn't seem to know anything about).

Rose had been surprised to find Prendergast's door open. He was most particular about his privacy, and had once shouted at poor Agatha for "snooping around" when she had only tried to do some dusting for him.

Now that Rose's eyes were used to the gloom, there was evidence that Prendergast had left in a great hurry. A still steaming cup of tea was on his table and a half-eaten bun lay next to it. Nothing would usually stop the greedy Prendergast from finishing off a bun once he'd started it.

Rose crept further into the room. Something about Prendergast had made her suspicious lately. He had been most peculiar about Papa calling in the police. Did he have secrets to hide?

She peered under a pile of coats at a box underneath, wondering what bizarre possessions he kept hidden away. Suddenly, she stopped still in astonishment. Surely she recognised that crate! There was no sign on it, no identifying mark at all – those had been scraped off – but to Rose's observant eye it was unmistakable. The size, shape and colour of the wood were exactly the same as twelve other crates that were piled up in the conservatory. It had to be the missing Chest 13!

Rose was about to rush off and tell her father, when she heard the front door creak open. There was a heavy footstep in the hall. Someone was coming towards her! She looked around – Prendergast mustn't find her in his room! What would he do to her if he guessed she had discovered his secret?

She looked all around for somewhere to hide. In a panic she noticed a long chest by the wall. She opened it and saw that it was almost empty, except for a couple of old sheets in the bottom. Having no real choice, she climbed into the chest and lowered the lid, just as the door creaked open.

CHAPTER THIRTEEN

Lying in the dark confines of the chest, Rose strained to hear what was going on.

"Where is it?" a muffled voice said.

"In this room... in one of these boxes!" another voice hissed.

"We mustn't be found here. And there's no time to check every one!" protested another voice. So far, none of them had sounded like Prendergast, but inside the chest it was hard to tell.

Then Rose heard something that made her heart sink.

"The Collection must be successful this time!" a voice declared urgently. "Leave nothing to chance... Take *all* of them!"

Rose fought back rising panic as she felt the chest she was in being picked up. She lurched from side to side as the shuffle of heavy, shambling footsteps confirmed that she was being carried away.

"Out the side way on to the cart!" a hoarse voice called

out. Rose was jolted around, she heard some clattering and crashing, and then everything went still again. In desperation she wanted to take a peek and see what was going on, but she found she could not lift the lid – someone was sitting on it.

"A job well done," a harsh voice croaked. "Let's move!"

There was a clatter of horses' hooves, and she was then being taken away – by unknown strangers who didn't even know she was there.

Rose clutched her moonstone tightly. It was all the more valuable to her now that the angel had disappeared, and it was the only token she had left of her magical visit to the Memorial Garden. Just holding on to it made her feel calmer – made her hope for the best, instead of fearing the worst. Suddenly it was as if she was looking on, from a distance, at an adventure happening to someone else.

"They don't know I'm here," she thought. "And there will be lots of chances to escape. I'm a spy hidden in their midst. I'll watch and listen and learn what they're up to!"

The horse clip-clopped along for about half an hour, then suddenly slowed down. The journey had taken them away from the noises and bustle of the city. Now Rose could hear only the cries of crows, and wind sighing in treetops.

"Open the cemetery gates!" she heard someone cry.

There was a great creaking and groaning as the sound of two iron gates swinging back could be heard.

"More deliveries?" came a voice. "Some folk think I must be running an inn, not a graveyard, what with all the comings and goings!"

"More work on the Great Tomb," came a gruff reply from the front of the cart. "Now let us by, or you'll be sorry!"

They rolled onward. A tomb? Rose wondered. Were they going to all this trouble of stealing the chest just to bury it? The mystery deepened.

Soon all the stolen boxes and crates were being lifted off the cart. There was a clinking of keys and rattling of chains, then the sound of huge iron bolts being slid back. Doors creaked and shuddered. Rose couldn't help wondering why so many locks and bolts were needed for a tomb. To stop people getting in? To stop dead people getting out? She shivered.

Now the noises outside were confused and echoing, as if she was in an immense vault. More doors were opening, as distant, secret chambers came to life, and there was a scuffling of many feet.

"Is this it? Do we have our prize at last, Collector?"

"Hands off!" came the reply. "Or you'll be for the Lime Caverns! You don't want to end up like me, do you?"

There was a chilly silence. Rose prickled with horror. What was so bad about ending up like a Collector? She remembered the odd men who had invaded her house. This had to be one of Hierophant Beelzebub's evil Mitten Men! Who were they? What did they want?

"Can't we just have a look?" quavered a thin wheedling voice. "Oh, go on! Who would know? Who would tell?" it added with an air of menace.

"I would know. I would tell!" roared the reply. "Now you and all your kind stay away from this little load – or there'll be trouble!"

There was a great rushing and flapping sound that Rose couldn't identify.

"All's ready! Open Imperialis!" came a command. There was a grinding of machinery, a whirling of wheels, a whir of cogs. A slow grating noise filled the chamber, as of a huge stone being lifted, then a blast of cold air seemed to rattle everything around her.

"Steady… steady!" The cries of instruction were torn away by a rush of wind. Rose's hiding place was put down again, on a surface that rocked back and forth.

"Down – all the way to the bottom!" came a cry.

There was a loud clang, a harsh ratcheting noise, then an awful sinking feeling. Soon only the echoing of chains and groaning pulleys could be heard, as Rose continued her journey. "Down into the tomb?" Rose wondered.

"But what kind of tomb can it be? I must take a look…"

Holding her breath, Rose lifted the lid of the chest open and peered through a tiny crack. It was very dark outside, and at first she could make out no details whatsoever. Gradually her eyes became more accustomed to the darkness. Then the truth dawned on her.

She was on a platform in a great shaft, slowly being lowered underground. Only one figure, wrapped in a cloak, was on the platform with her. It sat on the far edge, facing away, apparently lost in thought.

As the platform plunged deeper, Rose stared in astonishment at the vast underground world that was being revealed to her. She had read about mines in books, and it seemed they were descending into the most extraordinary one ever. She passed the mouths of shadowy caves and the crumbling ruins of ancient staircases. The weird squeals of bats wailed through the tunnels, sounding like tormented phantoms.

The figure with its back to Rose started to rise, so she closed the lid again.

There was a slowing down of the lift as it neared the end of its descent. Now Rose could hear water slapping against walls, gurgling and clucking against things in the dark. Splash! They hit what could only be an underground river. The platform bobbed around, then steadied itself.

There was a short wait. Then there were footsteps, as several people arrived to meet them. Rose wished she could look and see what was happening, but she didn't dare.

"You have been successful, Collector?" asked a voice. It sent a chill through Rose. She had heard its harsh gurgling croak before.

"It is here, Keeper!" came the reply.

"Then hand it over! What are you waiting for?"

"I… we… we had no time for a proper search, Keeper. So we took *all* the boxes in the chamber. The prize we seek must be in one of them!"

"Then you are not sure, you abysmal wretch? Stand aside and let me see!"

There was a sudden lurch, as a large heavy figure climbed on to the floating platform.

"It's here – it *must* be!" the Keeper roared.

Rose gulped. They were going to search the boxes.

CHAPTER FOURTEEN

"This one, master?"

Rose held her breath as a voice seemed to be coming from right above her. A hand touched the lid.

"Impossible!" came the angry reply. "We're looking for a carefully packed crate – one of a set! Any fool can see that's just an old clothes chest! Now, what have we here…?"

Rose could hardly believe her luck, as all attention was directed elsewhere.

"We have it! This is it! This is the one!" cried the Keeper. There was great excitement, as the mysterious robbers had clearly found Chest 13.

"I feel its power!" hissed the Keeper. "Call my barge – there is no time to lose!"

There was a sound of figures jumping off the platform as a boat arrived from out of the darkness.

"To Kensington Cavern! The great prize is ours!" called out the Keeper.

"What of the other things?" asked the Collector. He seemed to have served his purpose now, and was almost forgotten.

"They are worthless to us. Set them adrift in the Thames Tunnels – let the current carry them away."

Bolts were drawn by unseen hands, and the top of the platform became a raft. The Collector pushed it out into the river and the current began to pull it along.

All was silent, except for the drip of water. There were no footfalls, no voices, nothing. Rose breathed a great sigh of relief. She could hardly believe it. She had been set free – released with all the other 'worthless' items! Now was her chance to escape!

Making absolutely sure that the strange robbers were left far behind her, Rose stayed where she was while the raft bore her away downstream. After a while, one or two eddies rocked the raft so violently that she decided she would feel safer out of the chest. She peered out from under the lid, and when she was certain she was alone in the darkness, climbed on to the raft.

Despite the strangeness of her situation, Rose couldn't help but feel a terrible curiosity, tinged with awe, at the hidden world she had discovered. As the raft flowed along, she could see she was travelling through a complex network of underground canals. Judging from the ancient, crumbling stonework, they must have been built centuries ago, and now it seemed they were maintained secretly by the mysterious Collectors and their master.

Sometimes her journey plunged her into pitch blackness, but often, when there were meetings of waterways, and tunnels branched out in various directions, guttering torches would feebly light the way, or shafts of dim light from unseen openings far above would provide a glimmer of illumination.

At these turning points, there were faded and peeling old signs. Some were written in strange symbols that Rose couldn't understand. Others were in plain English and reminded Rose of names given to parts of the city above. Entrances to Westminster Canal, Piccadilly Pool and Great Tower Drains all passed her by.

Some of these waterways were rather too well-lit, and suddenly Rose felt anxious. She didn't want to be seen and captured, but likewise she didn't want to get back in the chest – she would never spot a way back to the surface from inside there.

With sudden inspiration, she pulled an old blanket out of the chest she had been hiding in, and wrapped it round herself. Now she might look from a distance like a bundled up Collector, on a mysterious errand. The blanket kept her warm, too.

Away from the strange robbers, more-or-less disguised, and now drifting smoothly along the river, Rose dared to hope that her luck was starting to change. She was peering ahead for signs of movement, when something caught her eye.

In the dim light she could just make out a strange sign of life in the dark hollows of the cavern roof. Above her, for as far as she could see, there was a great furry fungus on the ceiling. Then, as she watched, it seemed to sway, and wriggle as if alive.

She was astonished at seeing such a vast, hoary growth, stretching so far into the distance. It was almost like… Suddenly she gasped. With wide eyes she stared upwards and realised it was not a fungus, but a great flock of sleeping bats, hanging upside-down from the cavern roof. Far away as they were, and hidden in the shadows, she could still tell that they were bigger than any bat she had ever seen. And, here and there, long rat-like tails snaked downwards in the gloom. Cook's stories came back to her.

"Brats!" Rose breathed. And, frightened to move or make a sound that might disturb them, she huddled in her blanket, as the waters hurried her along.

As she went, she could hear faint squeakings and mutterings from above, whispers in a strange bat-language. She dared not raise her head, but she was sure that some of the brats were not really asleep, but having drowsy conversations with each other. She could almost feel her hair standing on end, as she was sure she heard snatches of real words, fragments of half-recognisable language from above. Could such things be possible?

The raft swirled around a corner and then, all at once, the brats disappeared. She had managed to sail right under them without arousing their curiosity. Once again she sighed with relief.

"Well done, lucky stone!" she thought. "Now show me a way out of here!"

The raft was floating towards a deserted-looking canal station.

"Strand Seepage. Metropolitan Underway. Change here for Fleet Flow and Lime Caverns," Rose read wonderingly to herself. As she was drifting past Strand Seepage, she suddenly saw a shadowy figure sitting in a dim alcove on the bank. To Rose's horror, it called out to her.

"At last – some traffic from the north! What's the news? Seems like there's something big in the wind!"

Rose said nothing, and hunched deeper into her blanket, hoping the current would take her safely past this hazard.

A second figure joined the first, and called out after her.

"Won't answer us, eh? Too good to talk, are we?"

Rose still said nothing, but she felt increasingly afraid.

"All right, you hoity-toity little creep! If you won't talk to us, let's see how you like this!"

One of the figures started to turn a big iron wheel attached to a shaft in the ground. There was an ominous sound of hidden mechanisms grinding. Suddenly a bubbling of water arose from a nearby wall, and Rose could feel the currents changing and pulling her raft around. With a sudden rush and gurgle, she was swept on a new course.

She sat competely still, hiding her face, as her raft now sped into a dark cave.

"Ha, ha, ha!" She heard a cackle of laughter behind her. "Shame you wouldn't talk. Now we've accidentally sent you on a nice trip into the Lime Caverns!"

Rose felt a chill go down her spine as the raft rushed along, and wicked laughter followed her all the way.

CHAPTER FIFTEEN

The Lime Caverns! What had Rose heard about them? Nothing nice, that was for sure.

"They thought I was one of them," she told herself. "They wouldn't send one of their own gang anywhere too awful, would they?" Rose huddled further into her blanket, hoping for the best.

A sudden rush of current sped her through the jagged mouth of a cave into a huge chamber filled with a weird light. Unlike the gloom of the rest of the canal system, this one was like a fairy-tale cavern, filled with stalagmites and stalactites, forming magical and eerie shapes of all kinds.

Spirals and whorls of twisting stone glowed softly in a million hues from vivid pink to luminous green. Some formations were like waterfalls frozen in time, or fantasmagorical displays of cake-icing gone mad. Others were more repellent, like crystal fungus, glistening blobs of slime in grotesque and monstrous shapes, or swollen growths over ancient wounds in the rock.

As she gazed at the shapes, she suddenly gasped in horror. Some of them looked human! Among all the unearthly shapes weird figures seemed to crouch, perfectly still.

Rose would have liked to turn and run away, but the drifting raft would not let her. As the current carried her close by, she could see they looked like fossilised men of stone. But what were they? Strange sculptures, or something much more terrible?

Some of the odd forms appeared to be solid rock – lifeless, cold stone. But others, staring blankly out at her, motionless under dripping trickles of limewater, were extremely lifelike, and looked as if they could arise at any moment.

Splat! Just when Rose thought nothing else could surprise her, a ball of fur crash-landed on the raft. It unrolled itself and spread out two gawky leathery wings, and a shrivelled little rat-tail. Rose was too astonished even to feel afraid as the pathetic creature peered up at her.

"What are you doing here?" it asked. Rose gulped. Despite her amazement and disbelief, she told herself she was in a desperate spot and had to think quickly.

"Important work," she said. The brat still stared up at her, as if she hadn't finished. "For important people," she added darkly. The brat made a thoughtful face, and chewed nervously at one of its tiny, sharp claws.

"I don't believe you," it replied in a rather bored way, curling up and perching next to her on her box. "You're going to the Light, aren't you? Will you give me a lift?"

"Yes," said Rose, trying to sound as if she really was a mysterious robber.

"You don't seem to be frightened of the Lumoren," remarked the brat, emphasising the strange word with special distaste.

"Of who?" asked Rose.

"The Stalagmen – our lime-pickled friends," He jabbed a wing at the ghoulish figures they were passing. The brat dropped his voice. "Actually, I think they're ghastly. Turning themselves into stone so they can live forever. Stupid idea. Don't worry – they can't hear us now while they're under the lime drip. They can only hear the stone talking to them. What does it say? Who cares? Still, quite brave of you to choose this route."

Rose stayed silent. She was frightened that any false word might give her away.

"Aren't you frightened of us wulpurgs, then?"

"You brats?" Rose asked, trying to sound offhand. "Actually, I've never given it any thought."

The brat – or wulpurg as it called itself – sat thoughtfully for a while. "You don't care, do you?" it said sadly.

"About what?"

"About me going to the Light."

"You can go wherever you want, I suppose," Rose replied.

The brat jumped up. "You don't understand, do you? I'm a wulpurg. If I go to the Light, I'll turn into dust instantly!"

"So why go?" asked Rose.

"Because I've been cast out!" the sad creature continued. "The other wulpurgs won't listen to me. They treat me as if I don't exist. So pretty soon... I won't! My name's Spiggy, by the way. Not for much longer, I suppose."

"Why have you been cast out?" Rose was curious. Extraordinary though it seemed, she found herself enjoying talking to Spiggy. All her life she had been fascinated by unusual creatures, and now here was one she could actually speak to.

"Look at me – I'm pathetic!" squeaked Spiggy. "I'm small, weak, I'm a scaredy-bat. All the others are getting ready for big changes. They hate all surface people. They say things are going to be different... now that *she* is on her way."

"Who's *she*?" asked Rose in a hushed voice.

"Don't you know?" asked Spiggy. "Well, perhaps you aren't so important as you think. Anyway, there's no place for someone as small and useless as me. They told me I might as well go to the Light. I mean, I hate Dwimolum – pardon me – surface people like the rest of them..."

Rose interrupted. "Why do you hate us – I mean them?" she asked.

"Because they don't stay where they belong! They dig under the ground, making noise and lights everywhere."

"You mean like building the new underground railway?" asked Rose, remembering Cook's story.

"Whatever the stupid thing is. But there's more. In the past there was day and night, night and day. It was fair. Humans had their time, and night creatures had theirs. Now they make big cities where it is always light. They have fires and devices to turn night into day – they chase away our beautiful darkness."

It was true. With modern progress, rows of gaslights were being put up all over the capital. Great companies in huge buildings all across London burned oil all night to get their work done. Even Rose could keep a lamp on in her room all night if she wanted to. To the wulpurgs this was all a terrible threat!

"Light takes away our secrets! It takes away our freedom. It kills us!"

"I see," said Rose slowly. She felt sorry for Spiggy and the other brats. "It must be terrible. The wulpurgs must be very afraid."

"Afraid? Hah! Nonsense. They're just angry. Angrier than I've ever seen!" Spiggy sighed and stared sadly ahead of him, as if trying to gaze into a worrying future.

"Humans will never understand us," he added wearily. "They don't realise we have as much right to life as they do. When they see us, they hate us and call us monsters.

"I'm sorry, Spiggy," Rose said quietly. "But I don't hate you – and I don't think you're a monster! I think all living things are amazing. It's fascinating to study them. Don't go to the Light!" she pleaded. "Stay alive and talk to me. Maybe I can find a way to help."

The raft was now nearly through the cave. The current carried it towards the last stone figure and Rose gasped. It had a face that looked familiar. White-skinned, shadowy-eyed, with a thin nose, bundled up in a great raggedy cloak and wearing shapeless grey woollen mittens, was... Prendergast!

She froze as, to her horror, his eyes suddenly flickered into life. A stiff hand jerked up and pointed at her.

"Rose!" he cried in an awful cracked voice that chilled her blood. The echoes of his voice filled the caverns.

Then the current carried Rose and Spiggs out of that ghoulish cavern, on into the next tunnel. Far off she could hear Prendergast's call being answered by thousands of eerie piercing squeals. There was a sound like a clap of thunder and suddenly a rushing like a terrible wind, racing closer and closer.

"They're coming!" screamed Spiggy, and then his little voice was drowned out.

CHAPTER SIXTEEN

Rose was terrified. She could hear the sound of thousands of brats pursuing her. The raft was rushing along in the blackness, but nowhere near fast enough for her to get away.

She looked around but there was no sign of Spiggy anywhere.

"Maybe he thinks I've got no chance of reaching the Light now," she thought to herself.

Rose shrank back as she glimpsed more trouble in the gloom ahead. Standing on a rock, right in her path, was another stone figure, rather small, but crouched as if ready to jump at her, its arms outstretched. She was trapped!

Then Rose gasped in astonishment. As she floated nearer she realised she had seen the figure before. It was the stone angel – the one that had disappeared from the Memorial Garden! Without really knowing why, she almost leaped for joy. The kind face she remembered so well looked calmly back at her. Its wings were now unfurled, fluttering and flexing with life. It was a miracle!

"Well done, Rose," a gentle voice said. "I knew you could do it – you're nearly free."

Just like the night when she had stumbled upon the little garden and instantly felt safe and calm, there was something about the presence of the stone angel that affected her again now. It flew over and joined her on the raft. The demented scream of the brats was getting nearer and nearer.

"Use the stone!" cried the angel. Rose had been holding on to her lucky moonstone the whole time, hardly aware that she was doing so. Now she held it out to the angel.

The little creature spoke a few words over the stone, then held it under the water.

As Rose watched, it glowed with a pale light, like a small weak moon behind a veil of night-fog. But then its power grew, and suddenly ripples and waves of moonlight danced in the dark waters surrounding them.

As the first brats wheeled around the tunnel towards them, they screeched with fright at the unexpected burst of light. They flailed their wings wildly, trying to turn around before the glow could touch them. But so many brats were flying up behind them that there was no way back. As the creatures tried to stop themselves, they began to collide, knocking each other reeling and dropping like stones into the water, choking up the tunnel with their hoary bodies and leathery wings.

Soon, in the magical glow, the canal was heaving with gasping, struggling brats. The sounds of writhing panic and high-pitched screams echoed horribly around the caverns.

"Will… will the light kill them?" asked Rose.

"No. Only daylight can kill a wulpurg. But there is a great power in the stone. It remembers light, if you like, from many centuries ago. That vision of purest moonlight threw them into a panic. But we haven't much time before they recover!"

Shivering, Rose peered at the half-drowned creatures, wondering what had become of poor Spiggy. Then the raft carried her and the angel round a bend and out of sight of the brats.

"We'll need some help to speed to safety on this raft," the angel said. "But we have an ally!"

He kneeled down on the edge of the raft and whispered mysterious words to the water. Nothing happened. Again the angel went down on his knees and repeated his words to the surface of the stream, this time louder. There was no result. Finally, the angel called out in a great voice,

"Father! I call upon you!"

Nothing happened.

"Hmph! Our ally appears to be asleep – or he's ignoring me! Well, there goes my plan for our escape. That does make this interesting…" he muttered to himself.

The raft drifted slowly until it reached a low harbour wall with abandoned barges moored against it, and a wide, dark pool. Above them a shaft led straight upwards, with a rusting iron stairway running crazily this way and that high into the gloom.

"Windsor Delvings," said the angel in a hushed voice. "I'm afraid this is going to have to be our stop!" Urging Rose to race as fast as she could, the stone angel flew ahead of her, fluttering hither and thither trying to spot enemies ahead or behind.

Rose had never been so tired in all her life. As she hauled herself up flight after flight of the stairway, she jumped at every distant squeal.

"Don't look down," urged the stone angel, alighting on a crooked platform just ahead of her. The iron landing looked as if it was about to topple over and collapse into the darkness below at any moment. The angel tapped the wall with a grey finger.

"Now here's something even they don't know about," he said. He placed one palm against the wall, and a circular section concealed in the stonework slid back.

Far below now, the brats seemed to be on the move again, as their jabbering squeals were growing louder once more.

"In here!" said her rescuer, helping Rose up into a narrow passage. "Old maintenance shafts, for the people who actually built this underground kingdom," the angel explained. "Our pursuers have only recently moved in."

When the stone entrance sealed itself up again, they were in total darknesss. The magical creature led Rose up and up, until she could hardly put one foot in front of the other.

Finally, the endless-seeming climb came to an end, and Rose was back on the surface. Exhausted, and almost overcome with relief, she threw herself down on the ground, blinded by the daylight.

CHAPTER SEVENTEEN

When Rose recovered her wits she saw that she had stepped out on to the roof of a peculiar stone ruin, a tower on top of a small hill, deep in a wood. Around them, dark trees creaked and huddled together as if exchanging secrets.

The stone angel disappeared into the tower, and came back with some water for her in a simple stone goblet. Rose never drank the water in London – it was foul. But she knew this would be different. She drank deeply and the water was indeed more delicious than anything she had ever tasted before.

Putting the goblet down, she felt almost giddy for a moment. She took a deep breath and looked out over the city. Something about the surface world had changed. Or was it she who had changed? Had her spell in the underworld affected her? In a strange way it was as if she was seeing everything clearly for the first time. She stared at the little stone creature, her mind full of a million questions.

"Who are you?" she asked. "What are you?"

The angel thought for a while. He seemed reluctant to answer. "It's a long time since I have had to tell anyone my name," he began. "I am not important. But I help to protect the things that are. I am one of the powers that watch over this Great Enchanted Land. We Watchers are many, from the lions in Trafalgar Square to Old Father Thames. At first I tried to protect you without revealing my magical nature. Such things are kept secret in these times. But you needed me in the end. Now you can call me Incantus."

"Have you been watching over me?"

"For a few days. Alas that I could not always be there when you wanted me. But I took a great step in trusting you with the Orbiniac – the moonstone. It has a special magic for providing strength against unknown dangers. There are terrible plans afoot. Dark things stirring. And you have your place now among them."

"But I don't want to be among them!" Rose protested. "I want to be safe and happy like I used to be. I want things to go back to how they were."

The angel pondered, his brow dark with responsibilities. He looked deeply into Rose's eyes, as if seeking the truth there.

"Things can never go back," Incantus said finally. "Do

you honestly wish you had never seen any magic? Do you regret having spoken to a little monster of a wulpurg and found him to be just like you? No, the only way to safety is forward – through the mystery."

"But do you know who the Mitten Men are? And why they want Papa's thirteenth chest?"

"It might endanger you to tell you too much now. But you remind me that there is much to do. Come, we must enter the darkness again, along safe ways that I know."

In the hidden tunnels under the city it was too dark for Rose to see all the wonders. But it was clear that Incantus was taking her along tunnels that were a further part of the mysterious underworld she had recently escaped. Here she glimpsed a vast monument, there a beautiful flight of stairs. At one point, in a still pool, she saw the reflection of an entire stone palace, like something from a fairy tale.

The drink Incantus had given her filled her with renewed strength. In what seemed like no time at all, they were ascending a short stairway. Incantus parted a curtain of dark purple leaves, and they stepped out into the Memorial Garden. With the angel by her side, Rose again saw all the hidden magic of the place, which had been lost to her on her previous visit.

"I should not tell you too much," Incantus said, "but when your father moved to this house, he brought a terrible magic power with him. What it is, and how he came by it, were not clear then, even to we Watchers."

Now Incantus was looking troubled. "Already I sense something has changed… The danger perhaps has moved on. Stay indoors, and be guarded by the moonstone. You will be safe for now, if you do not seek out trouble."

Incantus stood before her, pondering the next move. Suddenly a familiar voice made Rose jump.

"There you are! Oh, you have had us worried!" It was Agatha, pale-faced and trying not to sound angry, entering the garden by an almost hidden alley. Rose glanced at Incantus, and saw that he had resumed his pose as an ornamental stone angel.

"We've looked all over for you!" Agatha said, breathlessly. "We've had such goings-on! First Mr Prendergast's room is robbed, and he disappears – we suppose he's with the police, giving details. Next, we can't find hide nor hair of you. Then such a wonderful procession out of the house…"

"A procession? What do you mean?"

Agatha was walking Rose back out of the maze of alleys, round to the front of the house.

"All in good time, Miss. You did give us a turn, and no mistake. Now, wasn't it clever of Agatha to remember how fond you was of that secret garden you found? I guessed I might find you here!"

"Oh, Agatha! What about the procession?"

"Well, all those men from the museum came to help Professor Morrow with his work. Sir Gordon Bowler himself was at our door. You'd never seen your father look so proud!"

"What happened?" asked Rose as they entered the house. The hallway had a look of disruption; nothing was in its usual place, hatstands and chairs had been pushed to one side.

"Well, no sooner has Professor Morrow been telling us about his new job at the museum, and that good times are ahead for us all, than there's a knock on the door. Lo and behold, it's Sir Gordon Bowler himself, and a party of men waiting on him."

"Where's Papa now?" Rose asked.

"Don't worry, Rosie, dear. Just listen to this and tell me what could be better. The museum people was so worried with the tales of recent robberies at our house that they all came down in person to take Professor Morrow's fossils to the museum for safe-keeping. They didn't think all his collection worth taking. But oh, you should have seen them marching out of here with them twelve chests he was so particular about!"

Rose was strangely anxious. "And now? Where is Papa now?" she asked again.

"Why, he went with them, of course! About an hour since. Now, if you'll excuse me, Cook has left me about a hundred chores to do before supper time!"

Rose rushed back to the Memorial Garden, but Incantus was nowhere to be found. She looked around in dismay. Without her magical friend, she didn't know what to do. All she could think of was seeing her father again and making sure everything was all right. She needed to tell everyone that there was bad magic in the chests – but how could she make anyone believe her?

Rose dashed back to the house, but she stopped herself short on the doorstep. She realised there was no one there who could help her. Agatha would only treat her like a little girl and tell her not to worry. Rose decided that she would head straight for the museum and find her father herself.

"So there you are at last!" came a shrill voice from behind her. Rose whirled round to see a pretty little girl, slightly younger than herself. She was clutching an expensive china doll and standing beside a stern-faced nanny.

"You're the one who shouts at me through the wall," the little girl said. "I saw you yesterday from the upstairs window. Well, you'll be pleased to know that I've decided to let you play with me after all. Just don't touch any of my toys, and don't say anything to the servants. Now come along," she commanded. "Dolly is just ready to serve high tea!"

"Tea?" Rose almost exploded. "How can I think about

tea at a time like this? It's quite impossible!"

"Impossible?" the girl wailed in disbelief as Rose rushed straight past her. "But Dolly always serves tea at this time!"

Then she sat down on the step and burst into tears.

Rose didn't give her neighbour a second thought. After her subterranean adventure, the journey to the museum at South Kensington did not seem so frightening. Compared to caverns filled with screeching wulpurgs, the streets full of beggars and rude street urchins seemed almost friendly.

She entered through the iron gates of the museum and walked up the steps anxiously. Before she had had time to consider what she was doing, she saw Sir Gordon Bowler in the hallway, taking a carnation from a flowerseller and fixing it into the buttonhole of his suit. When he spotted her, he welcomed her with a smile.

"My dear, what a surprise! You're here to see your father, no doubt! Do come along – you never know, we might need your expertise!" he chortled, ushering her in.

CHAPTER EIGHTEEN

Stanley Morrow had been so thrilled by his change of fortunes that he hadn't minded for a moment when his Unknown Dinosaur was whisked away by the museum men. And he was delighted when Sir Gordon had explained that they would be taking his chests to the deepest specimen vaults for extra security.

He hadn't even thought it strange when, in order to get to the vaults, he had been led through a corridor that was marked 'Private – No Access to Museum Staff'!

But when Sir Gordon Bowler had sent him down in a lift-cage into the deepest cavern he had ever seen, and he and his chests of fossils were taken along a series of tunnels by shadowy figures, he gradually realised that all could hardly be well.

While one hooded man stood guard over him, he could only watch in astonishment as the other figures began to open the precious chests, and cluster around them, muttering. Professor Morrow gazed around the torch-lit cavern in mystification. Carved out of the rock, it was no rough cave, but almost a temple of stone. Arches and vaults of the grandest design rose up on all sides, to be lost in the shadows above.

For what seemed like ages, Professor Morrow looked on, frightened but fascinated, as his chests were all unpacked. Yet he had no cause to protest at the treatment of his specimens. Although the hooded figures seemed at times clumsy or cack-handed in their movements, Professor Morrow himself could hardly have shown more respect for the value of the bones.

Suddenly a familiar voice rang out across the cavern.

"Ah, Stanley! Welcome to a special meeting of the International Dinosaur Club!"

It was Hierophant Beelzebub. He was laughing coldly, and clearly not in any real mood for humour. Professor Morrow saw him striding ahead of a party of new arrivals in the outer chamber. Behind him, stumbling in the half-light, was Professor Lillian.

"Beelzebub! What on earth do you mean by this?" quavered Professor Morrow. "Lillian! Good heavens! Are you in on this too?"

Professor Lillian was not. "You might notice, my dear fellow, that my hands are bound, and that I have some kind of sinister brute forcing me along. I was lured down here by Sir Gordon, then these scoundrels fell upon me!"

"Silence!" roared Beelzebub. "You are here to work. I have need of your skills."

"I shan't do anything to help you, Mr Beelzebub. I've heard about you and your fanatical society of so-called Collectors. Stanley and I simply won't cooperate!" snapped Lillian.

Hierophant Beelzebub smiled nastily. "Oh, I think you will," he said softly. "When you see who else has come to help…"

Professor Morrow looked in dismay, as out of the shadows stepped Sir Gordon Bowler – with Rose!

"And if you don't think we are prepared to use… force, take a look behind you!" Mr Beelzebub barked. They all turned. He waved a torch, revealing a stone statue standing in an alcove in the rock.

But it wasn't a statue.

"It's… it's Old Jenkins! One of the museum caretakers! He's been missing for days!" gasped Professor Lillian.

"Yes," growled Mr Beelzebub. "He stumbled across our secret lift-shaft one day, and the Lumoren took care of him rather hastily. They have powers of petrification that can turn you into stone within seconds!"

Rose started to tremble. "You mean like they did to the policeman in our street!" she blurted out. "That's what happened to him!"

Mr Beelzebub smiled. "Yes indeed! Poor fellow, he was

stupid enough to ask our master why he was lurking outside your house, Miss Morrow! It was the last thing he ever did!"

He pulled the torch away from the horrible sight of Old Jenkins, forever fossilised, and led them on to the work site he had prepared.

"Consider yourself lucky, Rose Morrow, that you escaped from your brush with my Collectors! They saw some girlish trinket of yours that they took to be an omen against them, and took flight." He pulled a face, as if the memory of that failure was still bitter to him.

The threat of eternal fossilisation was enough to prevent any further argument. From then on, the experts bent to their work. Under the orders of Hierophant Beelzebub, and aided by the silent Lumoren, they studied the bones, great and small, and began to piece together the fragments of the creature like a giant puzzle.

"I hate to admit this," Professor Lillian ventured in a hushed voice, "but there's an extraordinary fascination to the work!"

Professor Morrow had to agree. For months he had craved the help and resources to reconstruct his Impossible Dinosaur and now, under the most bizarre of circumstances, he was doing so.

The learned men were astonished at the understanding and skill that Rose brought to the difficult task. She even told Mr Beelzebub at one point that he had put a bone in upside-down, and he was forced irritably to agree.

Rose watched in awe as the skeletal form of a vast creature began to take shape in that deep cavern. With the Collectors helping them, and with all the resources of the museum – wires, clamps and supporting frames – at their disposal, the work progressed with great speed.

"Wonderful, wonderful!" murmured Mr Beelzebub, as if this were the crowning deed of his life.

As Rose pieced together the bones, she glanced around her, hoping for some sign that the stone angel had followed her, and was looking on, ready to help. She knew the moonstone could frighten the Collectors, but without Incantus to guide her she didn't dare use it.

Her searching looks were in vain. She did notice, however, that there was one cloaked figure lurking in the shadows, who seemed to be more important even than Beelzebub. Hardly moving, yet always watching, he sometimes gave orders to the Collectors, who showed him great respect. Distantly she heard the icy voice, like grating stone, issue its commands. She felt a shiver, as she realised she had heard that voice before.

She peered more closely at him and realisation dawned on her. His slow movements, his great bulk, and his all-but covered face confirmed that she had seen him before.

"Mr Skellybones!" she whispered to herself. "He's the

Keeper! He's behind it all! And I know he's got Chest 13 hidden somewhere! At the moment the enemy has everything it wants! Oh, where is Incantus?"

Suddenly the work was held up. Professor Lillian was looking in disbelief at the bones he was now expected to add to the skeleton. He appeared to be frozen, unable to go on.

"This… this can't be," he protested. "Why, there must be a mistake. This simply cannot be right!"

Mr Beelzebub called a halt to the work. He called Professor Morrow over to him. "Well, well… the Impossible Dinosaur, is it not, Stanley? I believe that was to be the name of your lecture? And I also believe that there was more than one 'impossible' thing about this find that worried your scientific mind! Do enlighten us…"

Professor Morrow frowned. Although he didn't see why his discoveries should be revealed to Hierophant, he was too spellbound by fascination with his unknown dinosaur to be able to stop himself answering.

"Fossils are made in many ways," he sighed, rubbing his eyes tiredly. "But however they are formed, there is always a transformation process that preserves them. These particular bones, however, I would swear, are not fossils at all, but the original bones themselves, preserved by some extraordinary quality of their own. They are quite unique."

Professor Morrow's words met with an excited and approving murmur from the Collectors.

"Not only that, but all dinosaurs must date back millions of years. But the bones we have here are nowhere near that old. I would state with some confidence that the creature before us lived but a few thousand years ago."

"Impossible!" gasped Professor Lillian. Hierophant Beelzebub smiled.

"And," continued Stanley, "the question that stopped my colleague, Professor Lillian, from proceeding with his work is most astonishing of all. The bones he says we cannot fit on to the creature are the joints of colossal wings. No dinosaur this large could possibly have flown. No dinosaur could ever have had wings of this type."

"Correct," grinned Mr Beelzebub, "if it *is* a dinosaur." He strode up to the great construction whose immense sinister form was beginning to dominate the chamber. All eyes gazed up at it. "But what we have here, my dear friends," explained Beelzebub, "is a dragon!"

CHAPTER NINETEEN

Some of the bones were broken, and some had never been found - landslips and subsidences over the years had fragmented the skeleton – yet the shape now towering over them was unmistakably that of a true dragon.

It was a terrible sight. It loomed over them high and proud, dark fangs raking down from vast jaws. Spinal plates, like those on a stegosaurus, indicated a spiked and armoured back. With its mighty wings spread out, it looked far more deadly than any tyrannosaurus rex. Although those wings were only represented by an almost delicate framework of bones, they gave the creature a look of being ready to launch itself upon you in an instant.

Perhaps most disturbing to Rose was the skull. Dinosaurs had little brain capacity and were rather stupid animals. But the shape and size of the dragon's skull suggested intelligence. After her meeting with Spiggy and the wulpurgs, anything seemed possible to Rose. Could this creature have been capable of thought? Did it once even speak, to threaten mankind like the dragons in old tales?

That this creature of myth should stand before her filled Rose with awe. And fear. She somehow knew that this was only the beginning of some terrible plan. They had rebuilt the remains of the dragon, but what was going to happen now? She gripped the moonstone in her pocket and tried to call on the angel.

"Incantus – where are you? Why don't you do something?" she wondered.

Professor Morrow was still shaking his head in disbelief. He had puzzled over the riddle of his Impossible Dinosaur for months. Now that he knew the answer, he was almost dizzy with astonishment. But his first thoughts were for his daughter.

"I've got us all into this, Rose," he lamented, "with my poking and prying into the secrets of the Earth. Now we've disturbed something that should have stayed asleep for ever!"

Collectors began to shepherd them to the front of the chamber. Professor Morrow put a gentle hand on Rose's shoulder.

"Don't be frightened, my dear," he said. "They've got what they want now, so I'm sure they'll let us go…"

"Silence!" rang out the voice of Mr Beelzebub, as they were brought before the Keeper.

It was the first time Rose had seen him clearly. He was one of the Lumoren, a Stalagman like the figures she had seen in the Lime Caverns. Looking at him, she had to fight a feeling of revulsion. His face was like slimy grey rock. Dark eyes peered out of deep hollows, and his slit-like mouth seemed hardly capable of opening. When he spoke, his voice was like the grinding of rocks and stone in an icy stream – a gurgling, scraping sound only just human enough to be understood.

She realised now that it was the Keeper she had overheard when she had fallen into the old cellar the other night. He and a chief wulpurg had been lurking behind their house, making their plans.

Rose also noticed, as he motioned them to come nearer, that, like the Collector who had come to their home, some of his fingers had started to join together, fused by the lime-dripping process.

"The hour has come," the voice grated out. "You have served us well, in rebuilding Angarak the Last."

As he spoke, a Collector handed him a blazing torch, which he used to ignite a bowl of some strange dark liquid set before the skeleton. A column of fire blazed up and filled the cavern with a sorcerous red light.

"The Great Dragons ruled this land with terror from the dawn of time," his eerie voice rumbled. "They had more wisdom than men, more cunning and more desire.

So great was their reach and so frightening their power that man could only live beneath the ground, cowering, crawling for survival beneath the surface of the world. This underworld city, Englantis, is a relic of those ages.

"But forces of enchantment stirred to defend the land. Watchers and heroes arose, and in terrible wars one by one the dragonkind were slain. Angarak the Last was lost in battle centuries ago, and fell – no one knew where."

Rose stood spellbound. As the Keeper spoke, it was as if visions of cataclysmic wars between people and dragons appeared before her eyes. She guessed it to be the work of the moonstone. As she clutched on to it she felt it opening her mind, showing her scenes from a forgotten past. In the visions she also saw people battling against each other, humans betraying their own kind to fight on the side of the terrible winged creatures.

"You!" she cried out suddenly. "You were on the side of the dragons!"

"Hold your tongue, girl!" bellowed Mr Beelzebub. The Keeper shuffled closer to Rose. "She sees!" he gurgled, with a strange, sinister smile. "That is interesting!" Then, grim-faced, he resumed his tale.

"In the age that followed, men rebuilt the world and all memory of the wars was wiped out. They forgot the dragons, forgot this city, even forgot magic, or destroyed its terror by turning it into a tale to amuse children."

More bowls of fire were being lit around the chamber. It was becoming warmer. The bright fires were starting to become uncomfortable, like standing too close to the blaze on Bonfire Night.

The Keeper held Rose in his stare.

"But *we* did not forget. We sorcerers who fought on the side of the dragons, who craved their secrets, who longed to share their power. We stayed hidden from the new world that grew up on the surface. We entered the abandoned city of Englantis and waited for our time to return."

"But you speak of wars centuries ago!" cried Stanley.

"Indeed!" replied the Keeper. "We have made ourselves ageless with a cruel magic that gives us long life, while it slowly turns us into beings of cold stone. For centuries we have known how to preserve bodies, using the enchanted Lime Caverns. All around you, you see sorcerers from past ages, their servants and their slaves, living out the ages as Lumoren."

"In every age we seek out men of knowledge and ambition to aid us. The promise of magic power and ageless life is a strong lure!"

Rose glanced at Hierophant Beelzebub and Sir Gordon Bowler. They were now gazing into the fiery circle around the towering skeleton like men in a trance.

"Now I know almost everything," she thought to

herself. Then she blurted out, "But what about the thirteenth chest?"

Almost as she spoke, Mr Beelzebub, moving like a sleepwalker, was taking the chest towards the skeleton.

He opened it up, and they all gazed together.

"A dragon egg!" Rose gasped.

CHAPTER TWENTY

In the burning red glare of the towers of fire, the dragon egg seemed to pulse with energy.

"The secret of Chest 13!" sighed Professor Morrow, sweat now running down his face. "I thought it was the most perfect specimen of a dinosaur egg ever discovered. Even though it was petrified, I could almost imagine it holding real life!"

"How close you were to the truth!" the Keeper exclaimed. "Our lords, the dragons, are eternal, and they always find a way to survive. Angarak died in a great battle while protecting her only egg. Now we have it, we can call upon her magic power to hatch it!"

"But why do you need the skeleton?" asked Rose.

"You have heard, have you not, of such spell-weavings as 'eye of bat, leg of newt'? Magic power can be hidden in many ordinary things. Imagine then, the power that lurks in the bones of the greatest dragon ever to take flight.

"Now, no more questions!" snapped the ancient lord

of the Lumoren. "It was right that the story of our struggles be told on this day. But the hour is at hand. Remove them!"

Rose, her father and Professor Lillian were taken by the Stalagmen away from the centre of the chamber. They little knew how fortunate they were.

Around the skeleton the columns of fire were licking up towards the cavern roof. There were words of command from the Keeper, and a low, menacing rumble filled the air. The walls began to shake and splinters of rock tumbled down from high above. The massive head of an ancient statue, hidden for centuries in the shadows of the roof, came crashing down and shattered into pieces across the chamber floor. But no one was harmed – in fact the Collectors seemed oblivious to everything around them. Hypnotised by the fires, they stood uttering a mysterious chant as they moved closer towards the centre.

The skeleton of Angarak was starting to shake. Rose really began to imagine it would spring to life.

"I call the dragon-fire!" cried out the Keeper. There was a sudden roar and the columns of light surged into great plumes of flame. There were cries as Lumoren standing too close were caught in the blaze. Blackened, twisted shapes curled towards the ground, shattering into showers of cinders.

A fear that was both old and new stole into Rose's

heart. This was her first real moment of dragon-terror, yet the fear was ancient, buried deep in human instinct. Perhaps the moonstone gave her a touch of clairvoyance, for she seemed to see centuries of tyranny and misery stretching out ahead and behind. She had to try to stop what was happening, do something, anything.

She held the moonstone above her head, and was about to cry out when a stony hand grabbed her arm.

It was Incantus.

"I hope I am not too late!" he said. "I have spent my power talking with the Father, and have flown dark, dangerous ways to get here even now. But we are ready!"

He flew towards the skeleton. The glare of the fires was now too intense for Rose to look into it for long. Above the ominous rumbling and the the roaring of the flames she heard Incantus crying out.

"Stop this madness! You fools! Angarak hates human-kind! She will destroy you all!"

"She is coming!" the Keeper intoned. "Her spirit will breathe the fire of life back into her line!"

"Angarak is too filled with hate!" Incantus shouted back. "She knows she cannot live again. If you summon her, she would rather use her power to destroy us than give life to the egg. The skeleton must be unmade – the power must be broken!"

The Keeper seemed unable to hear. As the fires danced

and soared around the skeleton, Rose held tightly on to the moonstone for protection. Suddenly it was as if she could see the face of Angarak drawn in fire, flickering high above them.

Rose felt a presence entering her mind, a terrible human-hating passion, a desire to rule, a love of power. The dragon-will was descending on them all, as Angarak's spirit grew stronger. This was the power that had kept mankind in misery for centuries, an all-conquering will to enslave humans, to replace their gentle human emotions with the dragon-desire. This was the terror that had spawned such wars, such bloodshed, that all memory of those times had had to be erased by the Watchers, so that mankind could forget its nightmare and be free to live again.

For a moment Rose almost swooned under the might of the dragon-will. Then the voice of Incantus pulled her back to the present.

"We Watchers stopped you before, and we will stop you again," he vowed. "I call on the Father to awake!"

After Incantus's ringing cry had faded away, it seemed that nothing had happened. The fire still burned, the rocks shook, the face of Angarak leered out of the twisting flames, as the ancient dragon-spirit struggled to manifest itself.

Then Rose saw a dark shadow beginning to creep

across the floor of the chamber. From all corners it came, like black blood seeping out of cracks, rising from hidden pits, oozing through pores in the rock.

Her father bent down to study it. Then he looked up quizzically.

"Water!" said Professor Morrow in astonishment. "Water coming from everywhere!"

Turgid black silt slunk like syrup across the cavern floor and poured itself around the feet of the dragon skeleton. The fires hissed angrily and clouds began to boil around the Lumoren. The cries and agonies of the ageless ones filled the air in a scene of torment dreadful to behold.

What had begun as a trickle now surged like a flood. From the depths of the earth, water was sucked up, bringing curious creatures in its ebony tide, wriggling magrotten – like fat shining black millipedes – rolled in the swell, stinking sleeches, wrinkled ormlings and other creatures long forgotten by the surface world tumbled in its filth.

"Flee! The Father has answered my call!" cried out Incantus, pointing towards the canal system. "Go now! I will follow!"

They raced towards the underground river, which was now flooding its banks. But the landing was guarded – two Lumoren blocked their way. As they hesitated, uncertain, a third Stalagman appeared, carrying a huge club-like weapon. As he loomed towards them, Professor Morrow stood in front of Rose to protect her. The Stalagman swung his awful weapon back.

To their amazement the club came crashing down on the other Lumoren. Caught by surprise, they were beaten to the ground, dazed, and with a deft kick, one of them was dispatched into the river.

Their rescuer pulled back his hood.

"Prendergast!" cried out Rose and Professor Morrow together.

CHAPTER TWENTY-ONE

"You wouldn't believe the goin's on down here! Follow me, and let's get out of this hell hole!" Prendergast said, leading them to a long black gondola moored nearby.

"But you were on their side!" cried Rose in confusion. "And you gave me away in the cave!"

"This lot kidnapped me!" Prendergast replied, untying the boat. "Then the flamin' Mitten Men tried to turn me into one of them! 'Orrible it was! It was only the shock of seeing you that sort of snapped me out of it!"

"Explanations can wait," Professor Morrow said urgently. "First we must escape!"

Together with Professor Lillian, they clambered into the boat, which was rocking wildly on the rising tide and seemed eager to carry them away.

"I learnt a thing or two about this place, while I was sneakin' about pretending to be taken over. We need to take the left tunnel!" urged Prendergast.

He pushed the boat just in time. More Lumoren had

rushed to the bank to try to prevent them escaping. Prendergast's hands slipped on the pole as he struggled to steer them into the main current.

"Stupid things!" he cursed, and took off the mittens he had worn as part of his Stalagman garb and hurled them over the side.

"I'm human again!" he cried.

Suddenly they heard a long piercing whistle. Behind them, on the bank, a Stalagman with his fingers in his mouth was sending some kind of signal. It rang down the tunnels and echoed in the distance. From far away, they heard an answering cry – thousands of high-pitched horrible squeals.

"We're in trouble now!" Prendergast shouted. Rose's heart sank – she knew only too well what those squeals meant. Yet they had no choice but to go on. Rose took one last glance back into the great chamber. She could hardly make out any figures, just a nightmare vision of fire and flood, like a scene from the end of the world. Bubbling black murk and red mist, crackling with flames. Just for a moment the mist parted to reveal the fiery eyes of Angarak staring out at her, then the boat slipped into the tunnel, and away.

The waters carried them swiftly. For a moment Rose dared hope they might escape by some miracle. They rounded a bend, and there before them was a mighty arch.

"If we can get through there, we're away!" Prendergast said. Just then, Rose saw a little clot of darkness appear from under the arch. Then another, and another. As they gazed in dismay a vast flock of wulpurgs issued forth like a black plague, and massed above them.

"We have received the call… These are the invaders – cursed Dwimolum! Day-crawlers!" squealed one with bulging eyes and glittering fangs.

The wulpurgs hung in wait under the arch, as the waters carried the gondola helplessly into their clutches.

"Kill the surface-scum, the light-makers!" screeched another. There was a ripple of excitement through the great swarm; claws twitched and leathery wings uncurled, ready to attack.

"Wait!" came a sudden cry. "It's her! She is the one!"

Rose gasped. One of the wulpurgs detached itself from the host and wheeled in the air to confront the others. It was Spiggy!

"This is she of whom you told us?" quavered the voice of a very old wulpurg at the centre of the flock.

"Yes, Lord," said Spiggy. "The surface girl who doesn't think we're monsters and said that she would like to try to help the wulpurgs!"

"They must die!" screamed hundreds of the flock.

"Wait!" cried Spiggy. "She's the one who gave me hope! I was heading for the Light until I met her. She changed my mind. If it hadn't been for her I wouldn't have stayed in the tunnel after the terrible light struck us, and saved so many of my drowning brothers!"

"You did well, wulpurgling, and that is why you were accepted back into the Host. Do not undo your deeds now!" the ancient wulpurg croaked back.

"All of you – listen to me!" Spiggy begged. "Don't just follow orders! Think about the future – think about what's best for *us* for a moment!"

For a moment. That was all it took.

There was a cataclysm in the main chamber. A power that had been slow to anger had suddenly arisen in wrath. Floodwaters of incredible force roared down the tunnel towards them. At their head flew a stone angel.

"Father, protect us!" cried Incantus as he landed in the prow of the gondola just before the tidal wave hit.

The waters smashed into the wulpurg host. Rose screamed as she had never screamed before, as the gondola was hurled under the arch and down the tunnel with torrential force. Travelling at stupendous speed, the gondola surfed the colossal wave of black water. Broken bodies of wulpurgs careered alongside them for miles down the canal system, bringing wreck and ruin to everything they met. Only the little boat was untouched by the fury.

CHAPTER TWENTY-TWO

The raging waters finally began to lose their impetus. Man-made landings and stairwells gave way to natural shapes of rock. The gondola suddenly ground gently on to a bank of shale and they found themselves washed up in a cave, far away from the terrible scenes behind them.

Incantus asked Rose to produce the moonstone, and when he touched it, the white crescent glowed with a pure, beautiful light. In its halo, the stone angel surveyed the pale, tired faces around him.

"What happened?" asked Rose.

"Angarak is gone for ever," replied Incantus. "Father Thames came to our rescue. He was slow to anger and needed much persuading by me, but finally his magic won out over the dragon. The skeleton was smashed down and the dragon-spirit broken. The city of Englantis is cleansed now. Do not seek for Hierophant Beelzebub or Sir Gordon; they were in the main chamber when Angarak's power was broken. Nothing survived that cauldron."

"And Spiggy? What happened to the wulpurgs? Are they all… drowned?" Rose asked.

"I cannot tell. Though many of that breed are tougher than you can imagine. Perhaps the Father of the Flood spared that tiny creature, for your destiny was in his hands at the end."

"So who is Father Thames?" Rose wanted to know.

"The protector of this land. He is the Great River and a very ancient spirit indeed. Since the fall of the dragons he has had his mind on peace. He had almost lost himself in an eternal slumber when I called on him again. He has tried to forget war, as we all have. But this was one final battle he could not ignore."

"It's a bit complicated, Rose," said Prendergast helpfully. "But we was saved by magic. And the ghoulies have been washed away. I understand the general idea of it, it's just the detail I can't follow!"

"But I want to know everything!" Rose said. "Did you steal the thirteenth chest, or not? I found it in his room, Papa!" she told her father.

Professor Morrow and Professor Lillian had about a thousand questions, too, so Incantus said he would answer more, once they had reached a place of rest and safety.

Incantus led them along the bank to a slope where twisted shrubs and spiky thorns grew in the gloom. Soft mosses glowed in the stone-light and here and there clung tiny trees, hung with copper seed-lanterns. Half-withered, yet with a strange beauty, they bent sadly towards the ground.

"You cannot see it now because it is night, but these caverns have shafts that lead up to the surface. Just enough daylight finds its way down here to keep these relics alive," Incantus explained.

"Why are they relics?" asked Rose.

"They are trees and flowers from a different time," Incantus replied. "Many beautiful things that once adorned the land above are now only glimpsed in shadows in this underworld."

Brushing through some straggling gorse, the stone angel led them over the rim of what appeared to be a giant bowl, carved out of the rock. Water ran in beautiful patterns down into a central pool and flowers grew among the channels.

"Many wonderful things grow here, although many have died. Memories of the land that once was."

"A memorial garden!" Rose exclaimed, remembering where she had first seen the angel.

Yes – like our garden," Incantus smiled.

The delicious reviving water that Rose had tasted before was offered to everyone. Prendergast objected on the grounds that he had never drunk raw water in his life, but after seeing the learned professors take a chance on it, he did likewise.

Incantus spread soft, dry heather fronds over the stone for them to sit on. The glow from the moonstone was reflected in myriad tiny pools and the darkness was alive with magical light. Just to see this, Rose thought, made all her terrifying adventures worthwhile.

"The Final War had been over for centuries," began Incantus. "The Keeper hid in the underworld city of Englantis, searching, waiting for a sign that his masters, the dragons, had found some way to survive. Then one day, you, Stanley, discovered the skeleton of Angarak. When you brought together all the bones under one roof, the magic in them started to work."

"But why didn't it work when we were in Lyme Regis?" asked Rose.

Professor Morrow raised a learned finger. "You forget, Rose, that we didn't have enough room in our old house. The different parts of the skeleton were stored in various secret places."

"As I suspected," continued the stone angel. "Only when you arrived in London, where you planned to present them to the Natural History Museum, were they all together for the first time! That was when the old magic of the dragon bones began to stir. Strange forces must have been at work within your walls!"

"They certainly were!" Rose agreed. "I thought I was being haunted by dinosaurs!"

"The ancient forces were drawing attention to themselves. Angarak was calling out to any who might hear! The magic attracted dangerous visitors to your house, by day and night."

"Wulpurgs – invading our house to snoop around! And Mr Beelzebub and his Collectors!"

"Yes, all part of the same plot," Incantus agreed. "But one thing puzzled them. Where was the last, the most precious chest? Only one man knew."

They all looked at Prendergast. He squirmed like a guilty child.

"It was the horses that done me. I can't seem to choose the right ones. That's my trouble – not gambling, but gambling wrong. My uncle got me a job with you, Professor Morrow, as a sort of good influence on me, to keep me out of trouble, to keep me out of debt! But I owed such a lot of money I was in trouble with dangerous people. I 'ad to try to get some cash quick.

"Well, I was outside the 'ouse the day after you moved in and some geezer pulls up in a horse and cart. Says a box had been left behind from the previous day's removal job, because it was an unlucky thirteen. Could it be delivered to the great fossil expert Stanley Morrow, and was I him? Well, I couldn't resist the chance to lord it up a bit, so I

131

said I was!"

Prendergast looked sheepish and dried up.

"Out with your tale!" urged Incantus. "For your folly proved lucky for us!"

"I took the chest and hid it in my room in the old servant's cottage."

"Which was important," interrupted Incantus. "You taking away the egg meant that the set was not complete! The magic of the bones was separated from the power of the egg. This made it harder for the Keeper and the wulpurgs to act. It made them uncertain, which bought us time. It also confused the enemy. They were anxious in case it had been destroyed – or separated deliberately by one who knew of its importance.

"Until they could be sure of the truth, they held back. So they visited robbery and trickery upon the Morrows, gnawing away to get to the truth. Finally, and only when they were certain of the position of *all* the pieces, did they move in. Growing impatient with Beelzebub's elaborate ruses, the Keeper ordered Sir Gordon Bowler to use his position as head of the museum to take the skeleton away from Stanley. But continue, Prendergast, for some are keen to hear more of your story."

"At first, I was just curious," said Prendergast. " I'd been wonderin' how these dinosaur bones could be so valuable. And I thought, since everyone thought the crate had gone lost already, maybe I could sell it on the black market. I know a few dodgy characters. And I kept telling myself there's 'undreds of bones in the ground, and surely you wouldn't miss one or two.

"But I couldn't flog it to save my life. It seems you need very special buyers to be able to sell fossils. In the end I asked Old Methuselah who runs the pawn shop on the corner to put the word about in certain places that I had a special discovery on my hands. In no time at all I had a visit from a couple of mysterious blokes – halfway through me lunch I was – and the next thing I know I was being bonked on the head and carried away."

"Those 'mysterious blokes' were part of Hierophant Beelzebub's network of Collectors," Incantus remarked.

"Slippery villains the lot of them!" said Prendergast. "They made me tell 'em where the chest was. Then they dragged me down to the underworld to keep me quiet. They even tried to make me into one of them – said they needed workers. I felt like I was half-scared, half-mad and half-dreaming. Down in those horrible caves I lost all track of time, and even started to forget who I was. Then suddenly I caught sight of Rose – floating by on a raft through the Caverns. I called out her name but she was gone!"

"I thought you were raising the alarm!" said Rose.

"No, I just couldn't believe my eyes. It sort of brought

me back to earth with a bump. If I hadn't seen you, I'd probably still be wearin' mittens now!"

Stanley shook his head and smiled at Rose. "You have clearly been drawn into a terrifying adventure, my dear," he said sadly.

One final question bothered Rose.

"But what happened to the – "

"That's enough questions!" Rose was shocked, as Incantus almost snapped at her. Then he smiled.

"Surface dwellers back to the surface!" he said, and led them on.

CHAPTER TWENTY-THREE

"I went back," Incantus said.

It was a week later. Rose was sitting on top of the tower in the woods, where she had emerged into the daylight after her first escape from the underworld.

Not long before, she had felt the moonstone calling her urgently to the Memorial Garden. There she had met Incantus, who had brought her to the tower to talk.

"Down there?" Rose asked, with a touch of dread.

"Yes. Into the flooded ruins of Englantis I returned on a final errand. But first, tell me your news. What of your father?"

"He seems very well, thank you. Professor Lillian and Papa are firm friends now. I think their awful adventure has somehow joined them together, like soldiers after a war. Professor Lillian is awfully nice – he has given Papa a permanent job in the museum. He has his own office and everything!"

Suddenly Rose's face clouded over. "All the newspapers are discussing the disappearance of Sir Gordon Bowler! Papa and Professor Lillian decided it was wise to keep the true story secret. Was that right, do you think?"

"It was, and it was my advice. Magic is too dangerous a fire for man to play with. Telling the tale would only lead to the discovery of Englantis, the opening of the enchanted Lime Caverns, the destruction of the wulpurgs…"

"Then they aren't all destroyed?" Rose asked eagerly.

"No, no. I even spoke to a friend of yours, of which I will say more later. Don't be too anxious for Spiggy. A great disaster has befallen his people, but it does give them a chance to renew their colony, to change, to listen to small voices like his."

"So Spiggy is safe!" Rose cried. "I'm so pleased. I must see him again!"

The angel looked wonderingly at her.

"Well, you are a very bold young lady. I should have thought you would be glad to put your excitements behind you and never visit that dark realm again. Still, it may be that you will see him one day…" Incantus trailed off, mysteriously.

"Papa has found a thousand things for Prendergast to do at the museum. He doesn't understand the science very much," Rose smiled, "but there are heaps of things to be opened and sorted and cleaned and catalogued. It seems

Sir Gordon Bowler used the museum as his own treasure house. Hundreds of wonderful specimens were hidden in the vaults and locked away. Papa and Professor Lillian are working like mad to sort it all out. Prendergast is working day and night to earn the money to pay off his debts. Papa has been very good to him. He did take the chest, but he was very brave and helped us all in the end."

"Excellent," said the stone angel, but already his eyes seemed far away, as if on grimmer matters. A gust of winter wind brought the first drops of a freezing shower with it. He led Rose into the tower and sat her by a fire he had made for her.

Rose felt a slight quiver of fear at seeing the flames. The ancient dragon-fear had awoken in her when Angarak had been summoned, and somehow fire would never be something she took for granted again. She held the moonstone and in a moment she had recovered.

"I went back, because I had to go back. You know why, don't you?" He looked at her thoughtfully. "You were going to ask about it when we last met, but I stopped you. Some secrets are best kept as dark as possible."

He flew lightly up on to the windowsill and sat framed in the dim light, telling his tale, as the rain swept down outside.

"It is almost pitch-black down there now. The ancient torch-system that lined the canal ways was extinguished in the great wave. The water levels are still high, chambers and passages are flooded. All is silent, except for the endless dripping, echoing through the murk. A sad, abandoned, drowned realm it has become. Here and there, one or two frightened wulpurgs hang, huddled together in corners. They want peace and quiet now, not hatred and fear.

"I saw no Lumoren. Well, none alive, anyway. But the way to the enchanted Lime Caverns was blocked by a rock-fall, and it was not my errand to seek inside it.

"I was searching for the egg. As you guessed. I couldn't put the idea out of my mind that it could yet contain life. Many hours I spent picking my way through icy waters, fighting off the wretched magrotten and vile sleeches that came from the depths with the flood.

"Finally I called upon the wulpurgs to help me, and many did, including your friend. Spiggy was among the group that finally spotted it. The waters had swept it many miles from the main chamber. It was almost completely hidden in a drift of rank slime."

"So Spiggy helped to find the egg!" Rose said excitedly. "Where is it?"

Incantus flew down to a great bowl above the fire. It was completely covered with strange, crumpled, black leaves. They were warm to the touch and smoked gently.

Incantus lightly brushed off the top layer of leaves.

Underneath was the egg.

"I asked you to come here, for the time is at hand. Do you want to touch the egg? You will come to no harm. Not all dragon-magic is to be feared."

"Really?" Rose said, drawing nearer, "I thought they hated humans!"

"Only in the dark days of the Great Wars, when the cunning sorcerers inflamed their greed. But not all dragons were like Angarak. There have been others – oh, many ages ago – that were wise, kindly and great-hearted. Yes, in the right circumstances, a dragon can prove a friend to mankind."

Rose went to touch the egg, then pulled her hand back, uncertain. She looked at Incantus for guidance, suddenly strangely anxious. He took a deep breath.

"It seems Angarak realised she was doomed in the end. At the very last moment she did what the Keeper had wanted her to do. She breathed the fire of life into the petrified egg."

Rose leaned across and touched it with the tip of her fingers. It was very warm, almost hot.

"Oh!" she cried out, gasping, as a sudden split appeared in the top of the egg.

Incantus did not seem surprised. The crack grew bigger. A tiny green claw pushed awkwardly away at the cracking shell around it.

"Dragon mothers form a bond with their offspring, even before they hatch – a bond in the mind. It's a kind of deep, mysterious understanding. This... connection with the mind of the new baby comforts it and guides it before it has learnt to understand speech."

Now the shell was cracking apart all over. A bright golden eye peered through the hole the claw had made. Tiny, emerald-green, batlike wings could be glimpsed, pushing out through the splintering fragments.

"Now Angarak was dead and could form no connection with her offspring. It seems that in her very last moments, she looked out across the ruin of her hopes and chose another to take her place."

Incantus hesitated. He looked at Rose, as if hoping she would say something, but she was completely absorbed in the miracle before her.

"It seems that in the moment of crisis Angarak did not believe the Keeper and his followers to be worthy," the angel continued, almost with an air of apology.

Rose gazed in awe, as the tiny creature struggled up out of the debris of its shell. What astonished her was the beauty of the dragon: its colours, the rich patterning of its scales, the fine, sharp, spiky fins along its back.

"Rose? Are you listening to me? Do you understand what I'm saying?"

"It's a dragon! A real baby dragon!" Rose murmured.

Incantus put a reassuring hand on her shoulder and smiled a strange smile – part sad, part sorry, but with a touch of real wonder and delight. Incantus sighed.

"And, until it's old enough to know otherwise," he said, "I'm afraid it thinks you're its mother!"